Also by Michael Zadoorian

The Leisure Seeker

Second Hand

THE LOST TIKI PALACES OF DETROIT

the lost

TIKI

PALACES
of detroit

stories by
michael zadoorian

Wayne State University Press
Detroit

Library of Congress Cataloging-in-Publication Data

Zadoorian, Michael.
The lost tiki palaces of Detroit : stories / by Michael Zadoorian.
p. cm. — (Made in Michigan writers series)
ISBN 978-0-8143-3417-1 (pbk. : alk. paper)
1. Detroit (Mich.)—Fiction. I. Title.
PS3576.A278L67 2009
813'.54—dc22
2008037300

∞

This book is supported by the Michigan Council for Arts
and Cultural Affairs.

Designed by Brad Norr Design
Typeset by Maya Rhodes
Composed in Minion and Helvetica

For Miss Rita

contents

acknowledgments

The stories in this collection have appeared in the following journals and anthologies:

"To Sleep," *American Short Fiction;* "Dyskinesia," *The Literary Review and Ararat;* "War Marks," "Hearts and Bones," *Beloit Fiction Journal;* "The World of Things" and "Process," *The Literary Review;* "Mystery Spot," *Panurge* (UK), "Traffic Reports," *The PrePress Awards: Michigan Voices and Peregrine;* "The Lost Tiki Palaces of Detroit," *Detroit Noir.* The "West Side" prologue was published in *Massacre* (UK) under the title "308-810 (Dream Book)." The East Side and Downtown prologues were published in *The North American Review* under the titles "Camouflage" and "What Doesn't Go Away."

Great Thanks and Respect to:

Chris Leland; Sam Astrachan; Charlie Baxter; my editor, Annie Martin; my agent, Sally van Haitsma; Glenn Barr; my friends who have supported me for so long: DeAnn Forbes, Dave Spala, Keith McLenon, Lynn Peril, Tim Teegarden, Andrew Brown, Jim Dudley, Jim Potter, Luis Resto, Michael Lloyd, Terry Hughes, Gail Offen, Dave Michalak, Holly Sorscher, Tim Suliman, Mark Simon, Tony Park, Nick Marine (who *is* Tiki); my sister, Susan Summerlee; and to the memory of my mother and father, Norman and Rose Mary Zadoorian.

The Mauna Loa, Trader Vic's, and the Chin Tiki. R.I.P.

Detroit turned out to be heaven, but it also turned out to be hell.

Marvin Gaye

west side

after a plane crash, people in Detroit play the number of the flight, hoping it will come in. I have never done that, but after flight 244 fell out of the sky, I dreamed about it. Ashamed as I am to admit it, I looked up the dream in my "Kansas City Kitty Dream Book" and found that the number for Crashlanding was 606.

I played it straight for $3 in the Daily. I guess I could have played it on the street too, but that makes me a little jumpy. Just as well, because I lost.

I don't really play all that much. But some days I just see numbers everywhere I look—license plates, digital clocks, receipts. The same numbers over and over. If I see 872 on a truck, I'll remember that just an hour before, I got a receipt for $2.87. When that happens, I have to play it in the box. There's nothing worse than your number coming in, but in the wrong order.

Doing this, you get good with numbers. They become real for you. You know just what they mean, how far they can take you before you have to give up on them. (Like the number I cross off the calendar every night.)

My mother was the same way. Only she didn't give up on some numbers. She always used to look for my birthday on the bingo cards she chose. Then, after she set them up, she'd put lucky elephant charms all around the cards, along with a little embroidered picture of Mr. Peanut against a bunch of dancing numbers. "I'm A Bingo Nut," it said. She departed this earth playing 43 cards. The priest said, "She would have wanted it that way."

All I know is that it never comes in when I play Mother-562.

There's an old Polish lady I see almost every day at the drugstore where I play. Even when I'm there just to pick up some cigarettes or a quart of Mickey's, she's there. Ciocia Clara with her babushka and a wad of tickets in her fist. She must play $8 or $9 worth a day. She tells me her dreams and they always have her kids in them. I don't know how many times she's told me to play Stanley-159 or Katty-999.

Every week, I see Clara buying a "Skippy's Lucky Lotto Success Candle." Nothing but purple wax in a glass jar painted with money bags, a horn of plenty, and a big "Fast Luck" horseshoe magnet that uncrosses all the forces that keep you from winning. On the side, there's a white space about an inch square where it says: "Write your Desire Here." But it doesn't look like anywhere near enough room.

The drugstore has a whole section of good luck items—House Blessing Spray, Jinx Killers, 7 Holy Spirit Hyssop Oil. Once I bought a box of "DR. PRYOR'S alleged fast MONEY DRAWING brand INCENSE." The directions tell you to "Read Psalm 23 in the night while the incense is burning." They even give you a copy of Psalm 23 in the box. "The Lord is my shepherd. I shall not want . . ." etc., etc. On the back of the psalm is a tiny strip of paper with five different numbers on it.

The night I bought the incense, I had a dream about it. I dreamed that I had a step van full of incense and was driving down my street, delivering it to every house. They all had special doors in the back where I would shovel the incense. Then, the people came out of their houses and gave me money. I kept sneezing in the dream. I remember because when I blew my nose, what was on the handkerchief was bright green.

The next day, I played Incense-231 and lost $7. The number was 466. Just for the hell of it, I went home and looked up handkerchief. It was 646. At least that proves what I said about playing it in the box.

Sometimes when I open the dream book, I can't believe all the things people dream about: Slaughterhouse-104, Haberdasher-992, Fetus-369, Catechism-870, Grindstone-029, Herring-757, Thud-189. I guess the idea is you never know what you're going to dream about. Under my birthday horoscope in the dream book (745-957-842), it says: "Are neat in personal appearance. You value intuition more than intellect. You are willing to let things happen."

There have been times when I've dreamed about myself, Victor-987. I know it is about me because there's nothing else in the dream. I'm just standing there, looking at the top of my wrist, running my hand through my hair. I am standing and standing. It is the most boring dream. And that number just will not fall.

My wife tells me I am crazy to waste our money playing numbers. She probably is right. But she hasn't complained when a number of mine comes in.

One night, I had a dream where she and I were sleeping. I wake up and find some little animal running around our bed. I catch it in a sack and we both take it outside. In front of our house, there is a freeway. (This part is not true at all. I-75 is behind us.) I throw the sack under the wheels of a passing semi.

I never really knew what kind of animal it was, so I played Truck-319, both straight and boxed, and won $496. She didn't laugh at the dream book for some time after that.

Once in a while, I'll go to the store to play a number from a dream, let's say, Run-413. I get there and find two other people in line playing the same number. And one of them will know two other people who are playing it. I think maybe this happens all over the city, because in a couple of days, I'll see my number on the green sheet that lists that month's "hot" numbers. Sometimes, everyone at the drugstore is playing the same numbers, like we're all dreaming the same. If the number falls, the drugstore is handing out money all night long (not to mention half-pints of Boot's, Bar-cardi, and Easy Jesus).

On the inside back cover of the "Kansas City Kitty Dream Book" is a drawing that looks like it's from the 1940s. An old diner, filled with black folks dressed in razor-sharp zoot suits, with shiny conk haircuts. There are numbers everywhere in the diner—on the walls and floor, on a box of corn flakes, on the waitress's behind while she flirts with a customer, on the cook's hat as he scowls at her from his smoky kitchen, on the tablecloths and backs of chairs, even on the sign that says: NOT RESPONSIBLE FOR YORE HATS OR COTES.

I like this picture. Sometimes I look at it late at night in bed, when my wife has gone to sleep and I just lie there. I hear popping sounds off in the distance. I count the pops . . . 2 . . . 3 . . . 4. It's the bones in my knees when I bend down to pray, to write my desire here, to look for that damn dream book that's fallen under the bed. I like that picture. Sometimes I think about it before I go to sleep. Those nights when I go through the book, wondering what I will dream about, hoping for something. But those are always the times when I wake up in the morning and can't remember a thing.

to sleep

We come only to sleep, only to dream.
It is not true, it is not true that we come to live on the earth.

Netzahualcoyotl, poet-king of Texcoco

the walls of our Euthanasia Room are light blue, recommended to us by some people at a local hospice. The color is supposed to soothe the animals and I suppose it does, even if it annoys me. Light blue has always been my least favorite color. My mother used to call it "polack blue." Interesting, considering my mother was the all-time biggest, polyester pants suit, *deese* and *dose,* plastic-on-the-crushed-velvet furniture from Lasky's, Hamtramck polack. But I hate that color for different reasons. It's a silly color, insubstantial, frivolous. Yes, yes, I know it's the color of the sky and I could attach all sorts of glorious meanings to it, the animals are floating skyward to heaven, to a better place, *blah, blah, blah.* But come on. I'm killing these animals here. It's for a good reason, but I'm still killing them. Let's not forget that.

I can't do this anymore I can't do this anymore I can't do this anymore I can't do this anymore . . .

This is your litany while you lie awake at night. But you get up every morning, feeling worse and worse, and keep on doing it, until you start to wonder about yourself. Crazy things, like maybe you enjoy it, or maybe if you weren't doing it, you'd be packing an AK-47, the first woman to pull one of those fast food massacres. You can't understand why you don't just quit. You tell yourself you're doing it for the animals, but you can only tell yourself this so much before it just sounds trite and empty and meaningless. It sounds light blue.

Gilbert, my assistant, who suffers from dreams, knows what I'm talking about. He feels the same way. Except he likes light blue. At least it is a familiar color to the animals, he says. Out on the street, they look up and see blue. There in the Euth Room, they look up and see blue. It makes it easier for them. I tell him that dogs are color blind. He says it doesn't matter, they see their own version of blue. This is where I stop arguing. If you saw Gilbert, you'd stop arguing, too. The Man Mountain, we call him around the shelter. Gilbert's the one who carries the dogs and cats to the furnace room and lines them up in an orderly row in front of the door. A pile would be disrespectful, he says, and I would have to agree with him on that.

In Oaxaca, they have blocked off the streets. There are makeshift stands everywhere: small tented tables covered with bright flowered oilcloth, Mexican women rolling and baking tortillas behind them; men tending carts filled with huge loaves of bread blazoned with bones. The streets around the *zócalo* are crowded with people celebrating, but I'm heading for the grocery store. I have shopping to do.

When I walk up to the woman at the cash register with my phrase book and clumsily say, "Donde esta los perros y gatos?" she looks a little confused. I repeat, phrasing it a little differently. Still nothing. Finally, I give up and just walk around the store until I stumble onto what I am looking for. I fill my handbasket with cans. When I get to the cash register, the woman behind it smiles now, finally understanding what it was that I wanted. "Tiene usted muchos animales?" she says to me. I nod eagerly, and say "sí," not so sure of what it is that I just agreed to.

I drop off the cans at my hotel room and immediately set out again, this time for flowers. Marigolds and cockscomb, the traditional *flores de muerto*, are for sale everywhere, mounds of them, gathered against the stone walls of the marketplace, overseen by leathery, slope-shouldered old women. I have read that marigolds and incense approximate the smell of bones. Do bones have a smell? I don't bother to ask the old woman from whom I buy the brilliant gold and purple bundles. She barely looks up from her bowl of *pulque* to take my money.

The worst part is what we call "ghosting." That flicker in their eyes just a second after the Pentothal reaches the viscera, that moment, that last hundredth of a second of being as it folds into what comes after. The look in their eyes, during the wiping away of life, burns in on your soul like a klieg light on the retina. You can shift your vision elsewhere, but you still see the shape of the light, an after-image, superimposed on everything you look at—on a stop sign, on the page of a book late at night when you can't sleep, on your own guilty hand when you hold it before your face.

But unlike the after-image from a bright light, this one doesn't go away in a few moments. It's there for keeps. And after you eradicate a few thousand of God's living, breathing, sentient creatures like I have, you begin to believe that there's nothing left to burn. But you're wrong. There's always more work to be done, more animals to be put down. Before long, you're thinking that that part of you, the part your parents told you was what made you special, the good girl part, the part that would remain even after you died, is not yours anymore. It's just a charred, scarred accretion of the ghosted eyes of thousands of animals, the kind of scabby hard stone-cinder that we as children used to call a clinker.

In the village of Anenecuilco, the day before a child's burial, all the friends of the dead child come to play with the deceased's toys, while the body lies in the coffin. In this way, with familiar sounds coming from the other room, the parents can imagine for a little while that their child is still alive, giving them a brief respite from the pain of their loss.

Often, I will have to put a mother cat and her whole litter to sleep. We always take the mother first, so she doesn't go berserk if she happens to hear one of her babies in distress. The strange part is, while we euthanize the mother, the kittens are playing in another part of the room or even sometimes around our feet, chasing one another, tumbling around, so completely oblivious that it makes you envy them.

After the mother is laid down next to the furnace door, we do the kittens, one by one. You try to do it as fast as you can, working efficiently, mechanically, wrapping each one gently in a towel except for their head and paw, shaving a patch so you can find the vein, giving each of them their tiny lethal dosage, leaving your favorite one of the litter for last. (For me, it's the runt, the one that never got enough food.) You just do them and do them, till there's none left for that favorite one to play with. Then you do that one.

This is the worst thing that can happen: you do that last kitten, hold that delicate corpse in your palm, and you change your mind. You just plain change it. You want to bring that kitten home and you don't care if it is your seventh cat or not. *I've changed my mind*, you say, unsure of whether you've actually verbalized this or just thought it. Either way, you're completely serious. Then your assistant comes and takes the kitten away from you and places it over by the furnace with its brothers and sisters. They are all tucked against the belly, against the still milk-swollen teats of their mother.

I search for stalks of sugarcane, but no one seems to be selling them out on the streets. Probably because I'm in the tourist section of town. Still, I'm afraid to ask the people who obviously live here where they bought the long stalks that curl behind them as they walk along the *zócalo*. Finally, I find one man in an almost hidden corner of the *mercado* who sells me four of the long green stalks. He gives me a cool look, an American woman by herself, buying sugarcane. I wonder how I'm going to sneak them into my room. But back at the hotel, me coming in with armfuls of flowers and dragging four six-foot stalks of sugarcane, doesn't even merit a second look by the man behind the desk.

I'm sure the person who cleans up my hotel room after I leave will think I am a crazy *gringo* or *gabacho* or whatever they call Americans. It doesn't matter. I am appreciative. As long as the Mexicans let me use their world and their customs, just for a while, they can call me whatever they want.

Out again, in search of candles. Back at the *mercado* I find tall white ones, almost half the size of me; candles in drinking glasses painted with wild birds; small squat ones packed in what look to be religious Dixie cups, with the face of a woman mourner and the words "Cera Veladora Lux Perpetua" on the side. The only part of that I understand is "perpetual light." After I buy these, I notice that the wax is soft and greasy, and I start to worry that it is not wax at all but some crude form of tallow. At first I think that this will not do at all, but then it occurs to me that it will be most appropriate.

Finally, my shopping is done and I'm in for the night. Everything else I need, I brought with me from Detroit. Before I left, I went to a special store— *Skippy's Sacred Product Mart* on Six Mile Road.

Burn Incense Every Day For Lasting Pleasure. That's their slogan. It's painted in garish ghetto colors on the side of the cinderblock wall that faces their parking lot. Even though most of the stuff they sell is just supposed to help you win the lottery or keep your ex-husband away, they had what I needed. I bought three uncrossing candles, five packs of sandalwood incense, and a couple of cans of *Baby Skippy's alleged FIRE OF LOVE incense.* They also sold me a black cat bone.

On the long nights back home when I couldn't sleep, I read about Mexico and *Los Días de Muertos.* I found this tradition comforting. I liked the idea of being able to commune with my dead, prepare an *ofrenda* for them, ask them to come by for the day. I tried not to think about the fact that I was responsible for them being dead.

An ex-boyfriend of mine told me about *The Days of the Dead,* the beauty of them, the simple acceptance of death as part of the cycle, the mocking of death, because what was the choice? He collected the *calacas,* the little skeleton figures, and had them all over his house. They showed people performing various jobs, only as skeletons, as if whatever job you did in the living world was also what you would do in the afterlife. (For my sake, I hope this is not true.) He had an ice-cream man, a photographer, a barber, a secretary, a bullfighter, a mariachi band, all performing their duties as skeletons. He kept looking around for one for me. Wonderful, I would say. A skeleton woman with a big syringe putting to sleep little skeleton animals. He had a strange sense of humor.

Still, he didn't mind me talking about my job, hearing all the stories. That was always in his favor. He listened to me tell about my day, bad parts and all, which was more than most other people do, especially men. But even he expected me to turn it all off at a certain point, as if once I finished talking about a bad day, I was done with it and could go to sleep. The thing was, I was never really done. It wasn't long before he was the one doing the talking: the *why can't you ever think about anything but work* talk, the *why are you always so distant* talk, then finally, the *we have to talk* talk.

This is the dream: You wake up from sleeping and your hands are covered with blood. You get all scared and run to the sink. You try washing off the blood, you wash and wash—soap, hot water—it just doesn't go away. In fact, more appears from nowhere, then there's blood everywhere, on the sink, on the floor. And you're screaming and crying and still trying to wash, but there's nothing you can do. Soon, you're covered with blood, swimming in it.

It's a messy dream.

And not very original either, I'm afraid. I've spoken to other Euthanasia Techs who have the same dream. Gilbert gets it. I used to get it all the time, then one day, I realized that I hadn't had it in months. Then I had that to worry about. This is why: if you can do this job every day and it doesn't affect you, then you're not doing a good job. I don't mean the killing. It doesn't take long to become an absolute master at that. I mean that the only *only* thing you can offer these animals are a few hot dogs, a string of sweet hushed words, and a soft ride out, by someone to whom this matters. If you become a machine, you can't even give them that. That's the bind. You owe them your guilt. You owe them your dreams.

When I'm lying awake at night, I envy Gilbert his dreams, even the worst ones. At least until the next morning when he comes in to work. This is how I can tell when Gilbert has had the dream. First of all, he's late getting in. Second, the eyes behind those Coke bottles of his are larger and more liquid than usual. He looks like one of those sad big-eyed children from garage sale paintings. The third way I can tell when he's had the dream is because, well, he'll smell kind of bad. I don't know what it is, but you don't want to shower the morning after you have the dream. After all that blood, you might think that the first thing you'd do is take a shower, but it isn't. You don't trust water for a while after the dream. You don't even want to feel it on your skin. I have heard this same thing about junkies, that they hate the feel of water on their skin.

I start on my altars. At first, there was going to be just one for all the animals, but then I realized my error. Although I've seen many cats and dogs that have gotten along well, they are still essentially enemies. So there must be two. I try to construct them close to the ground, lower than the ones I have seen around town, so the animals can reach everything. I take two of the rubbery stalks of sugarcane and tie them together to make an arch against the wall. To that I tie cockscomb, baby's breath, marigolds, then crosses of beef bones and *nylabones*. I lay out a comfy blanket that I bought from a vendor. On it, I place deep pottery bowls of cool bottled water (my dead are American, and not used to the water in Mexico), plates of stringy darkred horsemeat from the stands at the *mercado,* butcher's mounds of ground beef, open cans of Alpo and Strongheart from home, as well as the Mexican brands that I purchased here. Also rubber balls, FlipChips, Frisbees, and knotted-up canvas bags for them to tug on if they're feeling frisky.

A long white candle in each of the corners in front, the smaller ones scattered around between boxes of Bonz and Snausages. I put as many photographs out as I could fit, ones that I have taken of the animals or cut out from our newsletter. And just as I have seen a path of golden marigold petals in front of many of the altars here, I sprinkle a path of kibble in front of mine to lead the dogs here from the land of the dead. There is also a pillow on the floor, if any of them want to rest after their long journey. And in the back, near one of the stalks of sugarcane, is a small red plastic fire hydrant.

At midnight, I start on the second altar. It is simpler than the dog altar because cats need less, prefer less. I wrap the sugarcane stalks around the only windowsill in my room and string it not only with marigolds and cockscomb but also with the catnip that I smuggled in plastic bags from home. I leave the floor bare, because it is still hot here in Oaxaca in early November, and I think the cats would prefer to stretch out and cool their fur on the tile.

After carefully positioning the candles and photographs, I lay out piles of

Kit 'N Kaboodle, MeowMix, dishes of salty ham, bowls of milk, and a litter box. Lots of cat snacks: Cluckers and Pounce and Bonkers. I hang hard rubber balls with bells inside of them and stuffed mice and strands of yarn. I open and stack bright squat cans of 9 Lives and Whiskas and Contento, make crosses of sweet dried fish. If I could find a dead bird, I would lay it there for them, then I would welcome the spirit of that bird to this room as well. But I'm afraid the spirits of all the cats would still be after it.

At around four in the morning, I finish the altars. There is something for all of them. I hope they will come. A ridiculous, infinite herd of them, a moving mosaic of fur and noise. They will be fighting like what they are, cats and dogs—barking, growling, biting, hissing, humping, sniffing each other's behinds, whatever, but they will be as they were before they met up with me. They won't be terrified, their arms will not be shaved and punctured, they will have regained control of their bowels, their eyes will shine with life again and they will eat.

I lay down on the floor to admire my handiwork.

The animals arrive. There are thousands of them, all sizes, breeds—Abyssinians, Poodles, Schnauzers, Siameses, and more Heinz 57s than you could ever believe. I never wanted to think about how many I put down—crazy street-wild, beautifully groomed purebred, scabby with mange, feral, piddled on the rug and I don't want him anymore, steel traps clamped to their legs, poisoned by a bowl of antifreeze the neighbors left out, in a home for five years then out because she didn't go with the furniture, thrown out of car windows on the freeway, genitals stumped off with pocket knives, we just got tired of her—unwanted, unneeded, beautiful, fucked-up, blessed animals.

I have always said you never forget their faces, but I have. A few of them look familiar, but most of them just have normal dog and cat faces. I realize that I don't remember them as living creatures, I only recognize them frightened, their eyes drained of life. The animals walk past and look at me. Some of them lick my hand and maybe whimper a little. They are not paying any attention to the altars, not enjoying the essence of the foods and toys I've left for them like they are supposed to.

They keep coming, coming, and I am still lying here on the floor. Eventually, they are not so orderly. I start to realize that some of them are not happy with me. There are ones that growl and snap at me and nip at my clothes. This is not supposed to happen. The dead are supposed to behave when they come back. After all, they're happy to be back in the earthly world for this brief moment. A Terrier with sarcoptic mange approaches me, then sinks his teeth into the soft underpart of my left arm. The others start in.

I wake up terrified, yet strangely refreshed. There is a wet spot on the floor where my face was resting, a few strands of my hair are stuck to the tile with candle wax that seeped down near my head. It is three thirty in the afternoon and I am really stiff.

After I wash up, I stay by the altars for the remainder of the day, burning incense, drinking milk, nibbling at ham and Milk Bones, staring at the candles, trying to keep the flies away, wondering what I'll do when I get home. Since I spent every cent I had to get to Mexico, I will probably have to go back to the shelter. But it is not all bad. There are the animals we find homes for, the sick ones we heal, the lost ones we return. As for the rest of them, the ones that will end up in the Euth Room, there is nothing to be said. I know they will keep coming and coming, without end, and someone will have to do my job.

The evening of November 2nd: I shoo them all home, back to the underworld, sorry that I couldn't light a candle for each of their furry lost souls. There in my silly decorated hotel room, I am the mummer. I play my boom box and dance—jazz for the cats—Louis Armstrong's Hot Seven, Monk, and Charles Mingus's *Better git it in your soul;* rock and roll for the dogs—Zeppelin, the Ramones, the Rolling Stones' *Can't you hear me knockin'*. I arabesque and twist and shimmy in black leather and a skeleton mask of papier-mâché with small pointed ears and a black snout.

There is a group of Maya Indians, the Zinacantecos, who believe that when we die it is not from any natural causes, but from the loss of our soul. To them, each of us has our own animal spirit companion, and when it is let out of its corral, our bodies, we die.

The Zinacantecos put their dead in a wood coffin, head pointed to the west, ready for the soul's long journey to *Vinahel,* the sky. Alongside the head of the deceased, a chicken head is placed in a bowl of broth with some tortillas. The chicken leads the inner soul of the dead away, starting it on its trek. A black dog then carries the soul across a river. The tortillas are his payment.

My book doesn't say what kind of black dog carries the soul across the river. It doesn't even say what river it is. But I'm hoping that it is the River Lethe, the one with the waters that cause forgetfulness, the river from which the souls that return to the living earth must drink.

When I die, I hope that black dog of indeterminate breed will have a soft mouth and will ignore my war crimes, see the good I tried to do, and yawn just for a moment to let my soul escape into the river. And if he does, the waters of oblivion will wash over my soul, almost pulling it into the depths, at the same time erasing all that I have seen and heard and smelled and touched, healing smooth all scar tissue. My soul will swallow, letting those waters of forgetfulness become waters of forgiveness.

My soul will emerge from the river, cleansed, beneath a bright blue, a Polack blue sky. It will drift to the shore, make a bed in the sand and I will sleep.

dyskinesia

james Topper had been doing a lot of traveling. He wasn't sure why he was traveling, but he was definitely eating well: fiery gumbo in New Orleans; dry-rubbed ribs in Memphis; Evansville, Indiana's squirrelly hot burgoo; cocoa-spiked Cincinnati five-way chili; as well as Buffalo's majestic chicken wing. Yet no matter how good the food was, he couldn't seem to stay in one place. He had lived in each place only about three or four months. The neighborhoods he stayed in, as well as the jobs he worked, got progressively worse with each town.

At the time, it seemed imperative that he just keep moving. James had left his wife back in Detroit and had heard that she was looking for him. Not to kill him, or even to hurt him, though sometimes he told people that because it sounded a lot more interesting. Actually, Tisha just wouldn't accept the fact that he didn't want to live with her anymore. It had finally, truly ended in Toledo, a town good for that sort of thing (and Hungarian hot dogs). James had been staying at a friend's place and she had caught up with him there. He was going out to get beer when she walked up to his car. He looked at her and sighed.

"Get in," he said. They drove to the Kroger.

Standing in the check-out line with Tisha and two twelve packs of Miller High Life, James saw a woman's magazine and right there on the cover next to a famous blond TV star was a big headline: CODEPENDENCY— WOMEN WHO CAN'T STOP LOVING. James picked up the magazine, handed it to Tisha, and said, "That's you." She bought the magazine with her own money and they both went back to his friend's house.

After James' fifth beer, Tisha pulled her nose from the magazine, looked at her husband, the huddle of beer cans next to his chair, and said, "You're right. It *is* me." Then she stood up, opened the front door and left without another word. Five weeks later, there were divorce papers waiting for James at his parents' house just outside of Detroit.

By that time, James was back in Michigan, up in Traverse City, staying with a cousin, wondering what he was going to do next. From all the moving, his car had taken on the look of one of those Salvation Army bins in strip mall parking lots. It was such a mess that he could barely see out the back window. He was broke, sick of working odd jobs, and had run out of people to mooch from. Besides that, the only local delicacy in Traverse City was fudge, which he hated. There was no place else to go but home, except there was no home to go to. For once, it seemed like a good idea to stand still. At least long enough to sign the divorce papers.

Not long after James moved back home with his parents, he met Madge. He was in the hot sauce section at the local market late one night, when he saw an older woman, around sixty or so, with long gray hair, braided, and wrapped around her head. She was trembling horribly, trying to reach for a bottle of Melinda's XXXtra Hot Habanero Pepper Sauce. One arm was held close to her body, her hand trembling in a way that looked almost exaggerated. Her head was cocked, as if continually nodding yes. James thought that if she got close enough to the bottles there would be a major accident—hot sauce everywhere, extremely *hot* hot sauce.

"Can I give you a hand with that, Ma'am?" he said gently.

The woman turned at him like a cornered badger. "No, you most certainly may not," she said in a low voice, almost a hiss. "I am not helpless. I can get a bottle off a shelf by myself, thank you."

"Sheesh. I'm sorry," said James. He grabbed a bottle of Caribbean O-SO-Hot Sauce and was about to clear out when he felt the corner of a shopping cart poke him in the back. He turned around to find the woman standing there, still shaking, but attempting to smile.

"Young man? I'm sorry. I didn't mean to be rude. It's just that people are always trying to do everything for me and it's much better that I do for myself. I really shouldn't even be here. I was just taking a walk and I felt so good I thought I'd just pop in here. I didn't expect there to be so many people. I guess it wasn't such a good idea."

"That's okay," James said. He was having a hard time not staring. Her head was tilted a little to the left and her arms were moving in a way that reminded him of Joe Cocker. Weird, considering that her voice and general appearance made him think of Katherine Hepburn. One didn't usually expect to find these two in the same body.

"Well, please forgive my being so testy," she said.

"No problem, Ma'am," he said, smiling. James pointed to the bottle of hot sauce that she had finally gotten off the shelf with no apparent damage. "That's some pretty vicious stuff you've got there. Have you had ever had it before?"

"Oh, heavens yes. I can't have it that often, but its good on just about everything."

"I had some last year down at the Jazz Fest in New Orleans and it took about three beers just to regain feeling in my tongue." He picked up the bottle of yellow sauce from his handbasket. "This is good too. Have you ever tried it?"

The woman's face was already slightly contorted, but she managed a small crooked frown. "I'm not all that crazy about those Caribbean sauces. They're a bit sweet for me and not quite enough heat."

"Oh," James said. This woman was no rookie. He tried to keep from looking at her hand. It was fist up, moving in front of her as if she were about to shoot craps. "Are you sure you wouldn't like a little help with your stuff?" James said, preparing himself for another outburst.

"I'm quite positive. By the way, I'm Madge," she said, holding out her hand. "No need to shake it. Just hold on."

He grabbed her hand and laughed. "I'm James. Nice to meet you."

They stood there and talked for a good ten minutes, discussing the merits of particular hot sauces (as well as the modern miracle of Pepcid AC). After a while, James was more accustomed to her movements and didn't notice them so much. He just concentrated on her eyes and on what she was saying.

"Well, I think you should stop by sometime for some of my famous jambalaya. I don't know too many people who have a cast iron palate like myself, so I'll make it extra spicy."

"That would be cool," said James, pretty sure that this meal would never actually occur, but appreciating the offer nonetheless.

James did know the house where she lived though. It was an old colonial a few blocks from his parents' place, right next to a lot where a house had burned down about eight summers ago. That particular night, he had heard the sirens and walked over to see what was going on. He remembered standing there, watching the fire, mesmerized: sparks rising erratically, mingling with the stars then fizzling out; waves of energy soaring nowhere, heat whooshing into the blue-black vacuum of a summer sky, distorting and confusing the night.

James did not even think of Madge again until one night a week later. It was about ten forty-five and he was driving around the neighborhood. He had taken to doing this most every night, just to get out of the house and away from his parents. He tried to be gone before the eleven o'clock news came on. Listening to his mother and father bitch about local and world events was actually tougher at the age of twenty-six than it had been at sixteen. Now, he didn't dare make a stink or else they'd boot him out. And since he only had an occasional gig as a grip for one of the local industrial film production companies (nonunion, which meant the pay was shit), that wasn't exactly a good idea. So at about ten thirty, he would get in his car, pick up a six-pack if he could afford it, or if not, a 40 of some powerful malt liquor, and just start driving around. Nowhere to go, so he just drove up and down the different side streets, trying not to go down the same ones too many times.

When he passed Madge's house, he wondered if it was a weird thing to do—stop in on some old woman who he had talked to at the market. But by that time, he had paused in front of the place and noticed that she was looking out her picture window right at him. It was dark and she wouldn't be able to recognize him, so she was probably ready to call the cops. Not good, not with open beer in the car. So James pulled over, got out, and waved at the figure in the window. He saw Madge cup her hand to the glass, trying to see what madman was visiting her at this time of night.

At the porch, James rang the doorbell and Madge's face appeared behind a small diamond-shaped window. After a moment, she opened the door.

"Well, I didn't expect you," she said. "I'm all out of my jambalaya." She was wearing old blue jeans and a baggy flannel shirt, her hair up the same way it was before. She didn't seem to be shaking as much this time.

"That's okay," said James. "I hope it's not too late. I was just passing by and thought I'd see if you were home."

"I thought you were a burglar, casing the joint."

James laughed. "No, I wasn't casing any joints. Not tonight at least."

"Well, good. I don't have anything to steal anyway." She narrowed her eyes at him. "Have you been drinking beer?"

James felt his face redden. "Well, yeah. Just one."

"You don't have anymore, do you?"

He paused to figure out what she was getting at. "Uh, yeah. It's out in the car," he said. "Want me to go get it?"

"Would you? I haven't had a beer in ages. No one ever offers beer to old ladies. They all think we drink Manischewitz wine."

"I'm surprised you don't just buy your own beer."

She crossed her arms, then uncrossed them. "Well, I don't usually drink. But I'm making an exception since I have company." There was a short silence. "You gonna go get that beer, or do I have to?"

"Okay, okay. I'll get it," he said, laughing, as he headed for the car.

When James walked into Madge's house carrying what was left of his six-pack of Stroh's, he was surprised at the bareness of the living room. There wasn't much furniture—an old easy chair, a couch, a beat-up school table—most of it covered with spattered drop cloths. In the middle of the room was a low-slung easel connected to a plywood platform. There were large metal clips mounted on it and a paint-encrusted shelf. It looked very solid, more of a superstructure than an easel. Not that he had seen that many easels.

What really dominated the room were the paintings. They were strange and coarse and everywhere—full of smears and splashes of color and raw-edged brushstrokes. Although James had never been one to look all that much at art, the paintings gave him a feeling of tension, of wanting to go for a run. It was like they were animated—though they didn't look like cartoons, or like people, or even anything he could recognize, but for some reason he thought they might start right off the canvas.

"Did you do these?" James said.

"Yes I did," said Madge absently, head shaking just slightly.

"All of them?"

"Guilty, I'm afraid." She touched the corner of her mouth, then looked up at a white canvas covered with swift bristling slashes of blue paint and diagonal yellow arcs that reminded James of falling stars.

"Wow. They're really . . . interesting."

"That seems to be the consensus. No one really likes them, but they all think they're *interesting*."

"No, I do like them. I just don't think I *get* them. Like this one here," he said, pointing at the blue and yellow painting. "What does it mean?"

"I don't know. I don't think it *means* a damn thing. I believe it is perfectly meaningless."

"Really?"

"Yes. In fact, that may be the sole virtue of my paintings. Their utter and complete meaninglessness."

James blurted a half-laugh. "Gee, I guess I can understand it then." He kept looking at the painting. The brushstrokes were like saw marks that seemed to slice through the canvas, through the wall. They made noises— crackling, buzzing, the sound of feedback.

Madge's head was turned to the right, her wrist twisted down against her stomach. She looked over at James, trying to catch his eye. "Say, how about one of them beers?"

"Oh, I'm sorry. Here you go." James plucked a can from the web that held the four remaining beers together, handed it to Madge, then took one for himself. "You've got so many paintings here. You must do this all the time."

"Every evening from about six to eight," said Madge. Her can of beer emitted a soft *pffft* as she slowly opened it. "That's when my dyskinesia is generally the worst."

"What's that?" James tapped the top of his can of beer, popped it, and took a long gulp.

"It's all this shaking and twisting around that I do. You know, what you try so hard to ignore? That's dyskinesia." She looked over at him. He was paying close attention. "See, I take medication for my Parkinson's. And there are times in the day when I'm pretty good, like now. But when my medication starts to wear off or I'm nervous, I get dyskinetic. The worst time for me is early evening, so that's when I try to paint, at least for as long as I can stand it."

"Wow, that's really cool."

Madge let out a short laugh. "Well, I don't know if that's quite the word, but thank you."

"Want another beer?"

"Um, not quite yet."

James started coming by Madge's house. It was something to do at night. He would drive around, drink a couple of beers, and then drop in. She was usually up. So they would hang out and talk.

One night, without even thinking about it, after the hottest gumbo he had ever had in his life, James told her about Tisha. Madge was surprised to hear that he had been married.

"You don't seem to be that type," she said. "I can't picture you settled down, working a regular job, bringing home the bacon."

"Neither could I," said James. "I think that was part of the problem. I didn't really know what I was supposed to do. I drove for UPS for a while, then I got laid off. After I started collecting unemployment, I didn't do anything. Sat around. Stayed up late. Drank a lot of beer."

"*Hmph.* I think maybe you drink too much beer."

"That's what she thought too. But after a while, I didn't care. I just wanted to be somewhere else."

"Why did you two get married in the first place?"

James leaned back in his chair, crossed his ankle over his knee. "Jeez, I don't know. We'd been seeing each other for a long time." He jiggled his foot up and down on his knee. "I guess we just did it because it's what everybody does. I guess it was pretty stupid."

"So what happened?" Madge said, her elbow moving upward in front of her.

"I went to visit a friend who works at a plant up in Flint." He moved his ankle from his knee and crossed his arms.

"And then what?"

"Then I just didn't come back."

"And that's how it started?"

"That's how it started." James tapped his foot.

A couple of nights later, James was getting into his car with a six of Motor City, ready for his cruise around the neighborhood, when he caught a knuckle on a bottle cap and tore a piece of skin from his index finger. He swore at himself, because it was stupid to get bottles anyway, cans were for drinking and driving, everyone knew that. He was sucking on the wound, when he noticed a cab pull up to a house across from the party store. It stood there for a full minute.

Finally, the driver got out, opened the trunk and pulled out something that at first looked like a lawn chair. When he unfolded the aluminum contraption near the rear passenger door, James could see then that it was a walker. A woman in her eighties hesitantly emerged from the cab and leaned onto the walker. The driver helped her toward the front door.

It was achingly tedious and James watched the entire thing, finger still between his lips, bitter, iron taste in his mouth. He watched her slow, brittle movements, the faltering shuffle, the cabby's arm cradled over the woman's hunched back, the one step after one step after one step. All the while, the blood was warm and acrid on his tongue. Finally, the driver got the woman up the steps of the porch and safely into the house. A minute later, he came back out, got into his cab, made some notes on a clipboard and drove away.

James kept looking at the house. After a very long time, a light went on in the front room.

When James got to Madge's that night, without even driving around first, she could tell that something was wrong. He walked through the door with an open beer, which he never did. And on top of that, he sat down and didn't even offer her one.

"What's the matter with you?" she asked, her voice more hushed than usual. "You look upset."

"Nothing. I'm fine," James said. "I just think I need something to do."

"Well, coming to visit me, isn't that something to do?"

"That's not what I meant."

"Oh. Well, what would you like to do?"

"I don't know. That's the problem. I know that I hate what I'm doing now. Being a grip is a stupid job. Move this, move that. It's busy work."

"You'll find something. You just have to start really looking." Madge's head was canted slightly, her right arm pressed tight to her body. "But you've got to truly work at it, because the world doesn't make it easy. Things just naturally move toward craziness, toward not making a whole hell of a lot of sense."

James put down his beer and squinted at her. "I'm not sure I follow you."

Madge took a deep breath and it steadied her. "James, just remember that you're talking to an old woman who was married for thirty-one years to an mechanical engineer who read way too much science fiction."

She took another breath and continued, her voice quietly deliberate, almost monotone. "It's the second law of thermodynamics, dear. You see, in an isolated system like the universe, all things tend to lose heat and energy, and almost always move toward a state of complete disorganization, chaos, and if you'll pardon my French, just general fucked-upness. You see? So right now, by sitting around on your duff and drinking too much beer, you're fulfilling your own entropic destiny. The idea is to break away from it. Defy that second law."

She looked over at James, who was currently staring at her with a vacant look in his eyes. "Oh, dear. I guess I've been rambling."

"I wouldn't call it rambling," said James, keeping a straight face. "It was more like taking a space walk." He started laughing. "But, that's okay. It was *interesting.*"

Madge squinted at James, stifling a smile. "Well, I'm glad you find me so entertaining, you little shit," she said, in her best mock martyr voice. "After all, I'm just trying to teach you something about the nature of things. But if you want to make fun of me, that's fine."

James grinned at her and nodded. "Okay."

One day, James decided to stop by Madge's house in the early evening. It was about six-thirty and he was pretty sure that she'd be painting, but he didn't think she'd mind. Besides, he had some fish sandwiches and a bottle of Cajun Chef green hot sauce that he wanted to try out with her.

No answer. He kept knocking. He knew she was there. There were lights on in the house and sometimes he could see some movement through a space where the drapes weren't quite closed. She was home. She just wasn't opening the door. He took his fish sandwiches and left.

That night, James almost didn't stop by because he was so mad. When Madge opened the screen door for him, she acted like nothing had happened. He just stood there in the doorway. "You know, I came over here today."

"Was that you?" she said. "I thought I heard someone, but I never answer when I'm working."

"I thought you'd answer for me."

"I'm sorry, James. At that time of day, I'm really not in good enough shape to go running to the door."

"I thought maybe I could come and watch you paint."

She made a face. "I don't think that's such a good idea." The tremor in her arm was getting worse and it was difficult for her to keep the door open. "Look, are you going to come in or not?"

James ran his hand through his hair. He avoided her eyes. "Naw, not tonight. Think maybe I'll just drive around for a while."

"Suit yourself," said Madge, as she closed the screen door. "But please try to think of somewhere to go."

The next night, James was back at about ten thirty with a six-pack of Pabst Blue Ribbon and a peace offering. When Madge opened the door, he carefully handed her a brown paper sack.

"Well, what's this?" she said, a little annoyed at him yet. She pulled the bottle of Manischewitz Loganberry Wine from the bag and started laughing. "Oh my God."

"I hope you like it," James said, trying to keep from breaking up. "Say, how about a nice big tumbler of it right now?"

"Come on in, wisenheimer."

They sat in the den and watched *The Great Race* on Turner Classic Movies. Madge said it was a silly film, everyone running around like a bunch of crazy maniacs, with no idea of what was going on. James noticed that her left arm and leg had a little more tremor than usual. Her left foot was twisted inward.

During a commercial, James turned to her and said, "Just think about letting me watch you paint, okay? I'd really like to see it."

Madge shot him stinkeye. "Now don't be a pest about that," she said, getting up to go to the bathroom.

The moment he heard the bathroom door click shut, James sneaked into the living room to look at the paintings. Lately, he had been reading an old art textbook from a humanities class he had tried at community college. James guessed that the book would probably call Madge's paintings *Abstract Expressionism*. He spotted one that he had not seen before. It was much uglier and more chaotic than the other paintings: long blots of red, black, and dark green—blood, bile, and mucus at once smearing one another, then pushing the other away. The painting scared James—It was like looking at a bad dream. He hated it.

Madge appeared at the doorway of the living room, arm bent forward at the elbow, slight tremor in the hand. Walking into the room, she suddenly stopped and James could see that her feet wouldn't move.

When he headed toward her, she gestured for him to stay. He stood there feeling useless. Her effort engulfed the room, filled it, as if with compressed air. The television chattered on in the den. James wanted to go kick it in, but soon he wasn't sure if he himself could move anymore. After another minute passed, she made a horrible animal noise and wrapped one hand over her eyes. Her feet seemed to loosen. A few small, shuffling steps got her over to a chair.

James rushed to her. "Are you all right?"

"It's getting worse," she said, panting, hands tight on both knees as if to try to keep everything from moving. "I don't know what I'm going to do."

"Madge—"

"Or rather, I'm wondering if I do know."

James' eyes and mouth tightened. He tried to get her to look at him. "What are you saying, Madge?"

"I'm saying that this never gets any better, only worse. And a lot of people decide that it's just not worth it."

"Madge, stop it. Shut up. Don't say that." He turned away, eyes stinging. The painting in front of him blurred, colors melted into each other—green into red into black.

She patted his hand. "I'm sorry, James. I'm just talking. You just caught me on a bad night. This goes through my head every day—and it goes out just as quickly."

James rubbed the heel of his hand across his eyes and headed toward the front door. "I think I have to go now."

Madge started to pull herself up out of the chair, then sat back down, exhausted. "James?" she asked. "If you're not busy tomorrow, why don't you come by at about seven o'clock? Wear some old clothes."

James was at the door, about to open it. He waved, but did not turn around.

The next day, James was on Madge's porch a few minutes after seven. He was carrying a pot of jambalaya that he had spent most of the day preparing. After knocking on the door two or three times, he heard Madge yell something. He couldn't make it out, but assumed that he was supposed to come in. Opening the door, he immediately smelled paint in the air, a clean thick odor that mingled curiously with the jambalaya.

In the center of the living room was Madge. Hair up, wearing a gray sweatshirt splashed with paint, seated uneasily in the big chair. It was covered with a thin, paint-crusted drop cloth. Sitting there, she looked like one of her own canvases, only moving—the colors on her limbs going every which way, sliding, crashing into other colors.

A few feet from her easel was a wooden chair, obviously placed there for him, yet he was hesitant to sit down. The worsened dyskinesia scared him.

Carefully, he placed the pot of jambalaya on the school table, and then took his seat.

Madge was saying nothing, mouth closed tight, lips squeezed to one side, her head moving continuously, not so much a tremor as just watching the flow, trying to keep up with the rest of her body. A small line of saliva sparkled beneath the right side of her jaw. She vibrated with uncontrollable internal energy—arms and legs doing a jerky electric dance—hand curling up around her head, flashing out in front of her. A wide brush was smashed into her fist, the way a person held a knife to cut someone in the belly. Sometimes she slashed hard at the canvas with ferocious movements, then just as quickly she would rock her body forward so the brush twitched against the canvas, trembling. The hairs of the brush would buckle, spreading the thin paint into small concentric circles. Often the brush rode right off the side of the canvas or missed it completely. It wasn't long before paint got on James, a long spatter of red across his neck and shoulders.

When Madge spoke to him, it was so soft and low, he could barely hear. "You've got to use it," she said. "Otherwise it's just wasted energy, nothing."

James looked over at Madge and she was crying. A few droplets worked down her face, between twisted lips. James suddenly felt as if he needed to leave, get out of there. But when he got to his feet, he just stood there and watched his friend: one arm curved up near her head, a halo of shaky bone and flesh; head down now in obeisance, both hands pressing the brush between her palms, a distorted invocation, asking for nothing but the next motion, wanting only to be there for it; each perfect move against the canvas sensing the chaos, marking the moment with an uncertain beauty.

war marks

the stain could have been blood, long dried and brushed away, or it could have been just one of those stains that appear on things you keep in the closet for many years, usually on something white, like a favorite dinner jacket or a wedding dress.

It had been so long I couldn't remember how the flag had originally looked. I know it wasn't clean. How could it have been, with everything I carried it through? All the mud on Leyte, the jump on Tagaytay Ridge, Luzon.

I still have a few friends from that time. I've been to the D Company 511th Parachute Infantry Regiment (PIR) reunions, each year someplace new. One year Texas, the next Arkansas, the next California. I'm still waiting for them to have one in Michigan. Just as well. Detroit is a strange place to be when you've fought the Japanese.

I talk to these ex-soldiers every year. Some of them I barely knew at the time, or even disliked. But now we are friends by necessity. Every year, there are fewer men than the year before. But there are always a few who have just discovered the reunions. They always have new stories, new details, new things you realize you haven't thought of in decades, all of it sparking new-old memories.

When I saw Johanovich, I went right up to him and started talking. I recognized him, even as an old man, from the photos we had tacked up. Sure as hell, he had no idea who I was, until I told him. It was his first reunion. He brought five Japanese flags, three swords, and his second wife. That's Johanovich. Evidently, the swords are supposed to be worth big money. I think he thought there would be someone buying them there at the reunion. He had already looked into selling the flags back at his home in Oregon. "They aren't really worth that much," he said. "But I thought maybe we could hang them up somewhere."

I knew about the souvenirs gathered during the war. My first glimpse of the enemy was of their dead. Jap soldiers lying in impossible positions; shirts ripped open, pants half off, slain and bare-assed in the mud. The flags and swords now hanging in rec rooms and workshops and finished basements and war rooms.

Johanovich is the one who told me about the symbols written on the flags. They contain information about the soldier. As soon as I got home from the reunion, I started looking for the flag I took from the body of my first Jap. When I finally found the thing, it looked different. I looked at the symbols smeared on it, and at the stain, and suddenly I didn't want to put it up in our basement. It felt like something I had misplaced for five decades. Something that didn't belong to me.

The Speak Easy Translation Bureau is located in one of those small gray or tan office buildings you can pass every day of your life and never notice. It's about five miles from the house I live at with my wife. One of their specialties, according to the phone book, is Japanese.

When I walked in, the woman behind the desk startled me. Her hair was ratted and teased and sticking out in big shocks, black at the roots, then bleached almost white at the ends. There was make-up caked on her face, with slashes of rouge at her cheekbones. She had painted bright red polish on her fingernails, cuticles, and the skin all around them, almost down to the first knuckle. Her mascara was black and thick, two eyes staring from the dark. She asked what I wanted and I just plain didn't know for a few seconds.

I unfolded the flag finally and kept my eyes on it while I told her what I needed done. They were not very busy today, she said, I could probably just wait. She slipped into the back for a moment. It looked to me like they hadn't been busy in a long time. The place was deserted. I sat down and read the *Detroit News* and tried to avoid looking at the woman when she came back out. I read a story about a fire in Wyandotte. A boy killed on his nineteenth birthday while making french fries.

After about ten minutes, a Japanese kid came out of the back. He looked like a college student: khaki pants and a pink shirt. The crazy girl at the desk turned to him and said, "This man wants the characters on this flag translated."

The kid looked at the bleached-out symbols on the flag, then at me, and said, "Okay, I'll do the best I can." He said it like he wasn't sure of something.

I read more of the paper (car accidents and more fires) until he came back, about an hour and a quarter later. He walked up to me, sort of cocky, and said, "Where did you get this flag?"

I looked up from my paper. "What do you care where I got it?" I said.

That flustered him a little. These kids see an old man and think they can say anything they want to him. He started to fumble his words then. My son did the same thing at that age.

"I was just wondering if it was from World War II?"

"It is," I said.

"How did you get it?" His voice was getting higher as he spoke.

I looked at him square and said, "I took it off a dead soldier's body." I was damned if I was going to lie. I did what I did. *Fuck 'em all but six,* we used to say. The ones that carry you out.

The kid looked at me almost frightened then shoved the flag and a big envelope into my hands. Taped to the envelope was a bill for thirty-five dollars. I paid Crazy Girl and walked out to my car, where I opened the envelope.

After I read the translation, I drove to McDonald's for lunch.

I have had people ask me what it was like to jump from an airplane. I always say the best part was getting it over with. To me, the whole thing was nothing but a series of shocks to the system. The first one being when you jump. Then there's a hell of a jolt when you come to the end of the suspension lines and your chute opens, and then when you see the ground coming up very fast. You realize that a piece of silk is the only thing there to save you, to let you float back down to the world, maybe not gently, but there all the same. Then it happens and you find the ground and are down hard and roll and get out of your chute and the earth seems like a friend who had gone missing, and now things are like the way they were. But then you look around and find you're in an entirely different place.

The soldier's name was Katsuhiro Miyazaki. He was from the town of Mugi, located on Shikoku, the smallest of the four major islands of Japan. According to my atlas, roughly 1,900 miles from where I killed him outside of Mahonag, on the island of Leyte in the Philippines. It was strange to find all this out about someone whose life you ended decades ago. Of course, if I hadn't killed him, I would be dead. I know that. Probably some of my friends as well. My children would never have been born. As for that Jap soldier, whatever his name was, I have no memories of his face. There was a uniform. There was a gun.

After I killed him, I felt only relief, hope that maybe I was strong enough or lucky enough to make it out of there and get back home. I may have felt something for an instant, but there was no time for it. More were coming and we had to kill them.

I called long distance to the Japanese Consulate to get the address for the City Hall of the town of Mugi. I wanted to write to see if anyone from the Miyazaki family was still there. The chances of this were decent, according to the woman I spoke to. It was a fairly small town. I had told her that I was trying to return a lost item.

To whom it may concern:

I am writing to inquire if the Miyazaki family still resides in Mugi. This family has to have lived there for at least fifty years. A son named Katsuhiro died during the Second World War. If this family is still living in Mugi, I would appreciate it if their address could be sent to me.

Thank you,

Carl Downhour

I enclosed a stamped, self-addressed envelope with the letter and had the whole thing sealed up when I realized it was all in English.

The same girl was at the desk as before. I don't think she recognized me, even though it had only been two days since the last time. She was a nutty one. She looked about the same, only this time she wore a light blue blouse with spots on it, from what I guessed was lunch. Told me I couldn't wait for the letter to be translated. I mentioned that I had waited last time for the flag.

"It'll be ready after noon tomorrow," she said.

The next morning, the *Detroit News* had a story about a farmer who accidentally slipped into his manure pit and was overcome by methane fumes from the manure. His son went in to rescue him and was also overcome, then a cousin. Finally, a young friend of the family went in as well. Ages nineteen to sixty-three, all of them collapsed into about eleven inches of manure. None of them got out in time. In the paper, it said methane is fast acting, odorless, and colorless. An invisible enemy.

I pointed the story out to my wife. "What a horrible shame!" is what she said.

By the time I got to the translation place, it was five past noon. Crazy Girl didn't say anything to me at all, she just handed me a big envelope. I didn't see the Japanese kid anywhere, but there was an invoice for thirty-five dollars taped to the envelope that was just like the other one.

Out in the car, I looked at the letter. There were a lot of symbols like the ones on the flag, only more distinct. They were linked snugly on the page. Some of them looked graceful, others dangerous, like something ninjas from the movies might throw. I sent it out airmail that afternoon.

Eight days passed and I got a call from Cass Wojack, an 11th Airborne buddy from California who hadn't made it to the reunion that year. He asked me how it had been. His voice was scratchy over the phone. I told him there were a few new guys from D Company, but that was about it. I told him about Johanovich, still peddling his flags and swords, just like during the war.

"Once a hustler, always a hustler," Cass said. We both laughed at that. He asked about the food.

"Better than last year," I said. "They had *Make your own sandwich night,* then *Fiesta night,* then the banquet on the last night. Everything was good," I said. "It must have been. Johanovich ate like a pig." Cass got a kick out of that one.

Then for some reason, I told Cass about what I was doing with the flag, that I was going to try to send it back to the guy's family in Japan. Cass' exact words were: "What the hell are you doing that for?"

"I don't know. I don't want it anymore," I said. "I can't throw it out. It's made of silk."

"Well then, damn. Give it to me," Cass said. There was some quiet on the other end of the line. "You're not getting chicken-shit in your old age, are you?"

"Fuck no," I said. "I still got my jump boots and my go-to-hell attitude."

"Well, hang on to those."

There wasn't much to say after that. I told him with any luck, I'd see him next year.

On the nights during a reunion, I sometimes dream about the Philippines. Not the fighting so much. I buried all that a long time ago. So deep, those memories only came back in my middle age, and then as war stories, with the same tone of action and adventure as the Doc Savage pulp books I read as a teenager. It felt good not to make them so real.

No, in my dreams are all the friends I had during the war. They are mostly in the same places as the snapshots I took at the time, the ones we now put up in the Hospitality Room at the reunions. They are doing the same things as in the pictures, only moving. Standing around, holding M-1's or Thompsons or squirt guns, looking tough, Pall Malls dangling from their mouths; shirts off, digging trenches; holding up souvenir flags. Behind them is mud or canvas or straw. They are all still alive. Some of the men were killed days or even hours after I took the pictures, way before I could pass the roll off to get developed. I remember thinking at the time, *They are still there on the film.*

I'm never in the dreams. I only watch, listen to them talk, think to myself during the dream, *Is that how his voice sounded?* or *Where was I when this was happening?* When I wake up I feel all right, I feel good, just not sure who it is inside this worn body. Sometimes I will even see one of the guys I dreamed about that next day at the reunion. I never mention anything.

After another three weeks, I got mail from Japan. It was just my envelope with a card in it, in both Japanese and English, with the name and address of someone named Kazuo Miyazaki. I had been waiting till then to figure out what I would say in my note. It had to be worded carefully, it seemed to me, if I wanted to get rid of the flag.

Mr. Miyazaki:

I am an American who served in World War II. I have in my possession a flag that was once owned by Katsuhiro Miyazaki, who I believe was a member of your family. It was retrieved in the jungle on the island of Leyte in the year 1944. Please contact me by mail if you are the correct person to send it to.

Thank you,

Carl Downhour

They were beginning to know me at the Speak Easy Translation Bureau. When I walked in, Crazy Girl was just sitting there, staring at the blotter on the top of her desk. Without even glancing at me with those blacked-out eyes, she said, "You want Ken? I'll have to check to see how busy he is. I think he can do it for you right now, if it's short." She spoke very fast, then disappeared into the back. I started to open the newspaper.

The Japanese kid was behind her when she came out. Crazy Girl pointed at me and said, "He's the one!" That sort of put me off. It was pretty damn silly considering I was the only one sitting there. The kid looked at me and when I met his eye, he looked away. I looked away myself, a second later.

I stood up. "I have a short note that needs translating." I held it out toward him.

"I'm afraid you'll have to wait until tomorrow," he said.

My hand just hung there. The paper was starting to wilt in it. "Fine," I said, putting it on the desk.

The kid walked out of the room without another word. Crazy Girl shrugged her shoulders at me.

I drove home and took a shower. It was bingo night for my wife and movie night for me. I was in the mood for something with some action in it.

I slept in the next day, made it to McDonald's just before they stopped serving breakfast. I got my English muffin and decaf and sat down to read the newspaper. On the second front page, there was a story about a man in Detroit, a guy in his mid-fifties, who drives to the medical clinic where he goes for back and heart problems. His car is covered with Nazi flags and swastikas, his face has paint streaked all over it. He's holding a rifle when he walks into the place. The receptionist knows him. She's nervous because of the rifle, but she knows the guy, she's kidded around with him. She says, "You know you're not supposed to bring a rifle in here. What's the matter with you?"

"I'm at war," he says to her.

"Who are you fighting?" she says.

He looks around and whispers, "It's personal."

Pretty soon there are police all over the place. The guy drops his rifle and tries to run out to his car. The police tackle him. There's a scuffle and suddenly this guy stops moving. He has a heart attack and dies right there in the parking lot.

I can't think of a worse place to die.

I didn't even get my free refill. I threw the paper away and just drove around till I could pick up the translation. When I got there, it was all waiting for me in a manila envelope. I paid Crazy Girl the thirty-five dollars and left.

After I mailed the letter, I forgot about it for a while. I was busy at home. Somewhere, my wife got the notion to redo the bathroom for the first time in fifteen years. I had been given orders to wallpaper. I worked in the bathroom while my wife washed down the walls in the dining room.

When I steamed off the wallpaper, I realized something must have gone wrong a long time ago. A problem when the house was built, when the wet plaster was applied, some sort of moisture that had seeped through. On the outside wall of our bathroom there were huge blotches, damp spots right on the surface. Then I remembered painting the wall a few times, trying to cover the spots, with the spots always returning, always bleeding through the new paint. I wasn't sure if I had just dreamed it up.

When I showed the blotches to my wife, she said, "Of course those are there. They've always been there. That's why we've always papered in the bathroom. Don't you remember?" I agreed with her just to quiet her down.

I repapered the wall and assumed I would forget again.

During that time, I received a new copy of *Airborne Gazette,* a little newspaper published by the same fellas from the old division who organize the reunions. It has photos from other companies' reunions, news about new members, obituaries, and usually some articles about the war.

There was a story about a place where D Company was stranded, late in the Leyte campaign. The guy in the story called it "Hungry Hill," but I'd never heard that. Ten days in the rain with no food, living in our ponchos. Most of us sick with dysentery and break-bone fever. So wet there, I kept a rubber over the muzzle of my M-1.

Finally, when the cloud cover broke for a short time, C-47s managed to fly low enough to drop boxes of rations. Us standing behind trees watching those crates slice into the mud. What the article had mentioned, what I had forgotten about, were the two men who were killed by falling C rations. I wondered what they told the families in the telegrams home.

Word from Japan caught me by surprise. It was a strange square envelope in the mail. My name was written on it in a scraggly, stick-figure printing style that I still sometimes see on old steamer trunks in junk shops. Opening the letter, the paper felt different to me, coarse.

Mr. Downhour:

Please forgive language of this message. A friend is giving translation. I would be pleased to receive flag of Katsuhiro Miyazaki. He was uncle of mine I have never met. Please how did you receive his flag? Why are you returning?

With thanks,

Kazuo Miyazaki

I read the note a few times. It was clumsy, but I knew what it was saying. At that point, it had been well over two months since I had started the whole thing. Part of me had gotten real tired of it. Not to mention the expense. My wife was asking questions. How was I going through my house allowance so quickly? I told her it was for something I was working on down in my shop. It was costing more than I thought to finish.

Mr. Miyazaki:

I regret to inform you that I am responsible for your uncle's death in December 1944 near Mahonag on the island of Leyte in the Philippines. I took the flag from his body. I am returning it because it belongs to your family. The flag is enclosed.

Respectfully,

Carl Downhour

There was a new girl at the Speak Easy Translation Bureau, a little brunette who looked like she might have been just out of college. She was on the phone when I came in. When I spoke to her, she tilted the receiver away from her face and clasped her hand over the mouthpiece. I told her that I wanted a letter translated. She said she was just a temp, handling the phones. Had I been there before? Could I do it myself?

"If I could do it myself, I wouldn't be here." She giggled at that. "Sure, I'll take care of it," I said. I walked toward the room where I had seen the Japanese kid come from during my other visits.

He was in there sitting at the table, eating his lunch. His back was to me, but I knew it was a peanut butter and jelly sandwich. I've made enough of them in my life to recognize the smell.

"I'd like you to translate this for me," I said. His head went erect. I could tell I'd startled him. He must have put his sandwich down before turning around because he took a while to face me. When he did, he looked right at me like he had been getting ready for it. He wiped his fingers with a wadded-up paper napkin before taking the letter from me.

"I probably won't be able to get to this until late in the afternoon, or even tomorrow," he said, in a hurry to get it out.

I was about to say fine, when I saw him start to read the letter. I should have left then and there, but I didn't. I watched him read it. When he was done, he looked back up at me and said, "I'll do this for you right now. You can wait in the other room."

I stood there without saying anything, then wandered back to the waiting room. The new girl was there, still on the phone, jabbering away at someone. I took off my hat and sat down. Since I had forgotten my newspaper, there was nothing to look at except for an old *Reader's Digest.* The only interesting story was about a man who was revived after receiving a prolonged electrical shock from a household appliance.

About forty-five minutes later, the kid came out and handed me every-thing. It wasn't all neat in an envelope like before. "It's all set," he said. There was the start of a smile on his face.

"Thank you," I said. I was having a problem meeting his eyes. Then I met them and that was that.

"I think what you're doing is good," he said.

I stood, picked up my hat. "You don't know a thing about it," I said. "And even if you did, it would be none of your business."

He maybe was going to say something else, but then he turned and went into the other room. I noticed he hadn't given me a bill.

I looked at the translated letter, at the tiny smear of peanut butter on the margin. Finally, I turned around myself, got the girl's attention, and paid my thirty-five dollars.

the world of things

In space things touch. In time things part.

E. M. Forster

my house is filled with objects taken from my parents' house and other parents' houses, perhaps yours. I have a particular taste for the items of the early sixties, that era when my parents were in their prime: good white middle-class folks living in a good white middle-class Detroit neighborhood. The objects they possessed are what obsess me now—things Danish Modern and Limed Oak, things Lucite and mosaic, things flecked and swirled with ovoid Jet Age patterns, things ludicrously self-serious with their commitment to the well-living of the American dream.

Of course, the American dream changed in Detroit after the '67 riots. Lots of those good white middle-class folks headed north of 8 Mile Road afterward and just kept on going into the suburbs and beyond. Mine didn't. Yet I'm not that different from the other riot babies born that year, a bit daffier perhaps, a bit more forward in my obsession. We are the ones who still watch the old television shows on cable, that crave our "comfort foods," that buy the resurrected Mustangs, Chargers, and GTOs that the Big Three is currently retrofitting for us. Yet those same folks come over to my house and smile bemusedly at my "collection." But I don't *collect* these things, I simply like them. I read somewhere that we are all secretly enamored of the decade in which we are born. That is certainly the case with me.

In the late eighties, I picked up a few items at a thrift shop to fill my bachelor's apartment: boomerang Formica kitchen table, tubular chrome kitchen chairs, a cowboy couch with wagon-wheel arms and six-guns embroidered into the cushions. I can't say what attracted me to them. After that, I happened upon a few other items—mosaic cityscapes, blond end tables, a streamlined Toastmaster. Before long I was scouring garage sales, thrift stores, and estate sales (not to mention mom and dad's living room) for the detritus of my elders' glory days—bilevel coffee tables, tiki mugs, Russel Wright dinnerware, letter holders that looked like dachshunds, wild geometric-patterned drapes, hi-fi albums with music that percolated between speakers, coat racks that resembled atomic molecules.

I wanted to live in a "Rumpus Room."

I got a job in advertising as an art director and in the Creative Department, discovered other people who shared my tastes. Each grateful for the other's peculiarity, we huddled in offices sharing information about estate sales, devouring books of fifties and sixties design as if it were samizdat. We loved it all—automobiles, diners, lamps, matchbook covers, furniture, corporate logos. We laughed knowingly at the amoeba fabrics, Harley Earl's bosomy automotive appendages, the super-saturated color photographs of aproned suburban Dads in their backyards wielding freshly grilled wieners. Yet I also believe there was a genuine affection for what we saw, even while recognizing our own twisted longings for some romanticized, sanitized America that never existed, and that we would have hated had we been forced to live there as adults. Still, I decided that I never wanted to live in a home furnished with *regular* things—beige plaid couches, entertainment centers, wall-to-wall carpeting, and such. I had friends from my college years who lived in those kinds of Scotchgarded, childproof, generic homes. Over time, I lost touch with all of them.

I met Grazyna at one of the agencies I worked at, and though her interest in old things never matched mine, being near someone like me intensified her appreciation. We married and as soon as we could, we bought a house and I filled it with these foolish things, the things our parents embraced, then outgrew, then expunged.

But not my mother, who continued to live in that good middle-class neighborhood even after it became a neighborhood of crack houses—main streets lined with the faded exoskeletons of burned-out mom-and-pop stores and boarded-up car dealerships with weeds growing between the concrete slabs where bright Chryslers once stood. This is where she and my father lived for thirty-seven years, where my mother lived the last eight years of her life before she died two weeks ago. It is where she kept a basement full of treasures from my childhood, things she wouldn't let me have, or even look at, no matter how much I begged.

You'd think that she might have been amused by her son's offbeat tastes, but that was not the case. Could it have been because I kept coming over to her house and asking for everything? Perhaps. But the truth is that she stopped liking everything, including herself, sometime in the seventies. She hated getting "old" and took it out on the times. Later, you could mention all that post-Kennedy America's loss of innocence stuff to her, but she would just snarl and say that the people back then were better groomed and a lot less likely to shoot you. In the eighties, she became bitter and there was nothing my father or I could do about it. In the nineties, my father died and that just made her worse.

The neighborhood got dangerous and I repeatedly asked her to move, assuring her of financial help and total independence, hoping primarily to keep her safe, of course, but in the far reaches of my mind thinking that maybe I could finally get my hands on the basement things she had closed off to me. But she remained in the old house, living behind protective grating, reinforced dead bolts, and an alarm system that automatically contacted police in case of intruders. I now realize that what really protected her were all those things from her life with my father, those same things that my friends and I snigger over campishly. But now that she is dead, I find it hard to be amused.

At the house, Grazyna and I lock the Mustang, activate the alarm, and walk briskly to the house, cautious white folks that we are, softened by years of suburban life, aware that our mere lack of pigmentation may be cause for racial unrest. We lock ourselves in, slamming shut the protective grill behind us. I pray for no sudden conflagrations, because engaging and disengaging this cage door confuses me and I, master of the worst case scenario, who always spots the accident before it happens (much to Grazyna's amusement), have a vision of the two of us trapped in my mother's house, char-broiled over flaming kitsch.

"Oh my God," Grazyna says as we enter the living room.

She has obviously forgotten just how much junk, and I do mean junk, my mother had. Grazyna hasn't been to the house in years. On holidays, it was my job to pick up my mother and take her to our place. When I visited, I came by myself. Grazyna is a strong-willed woman and so was my mother, so you can guess the rest. No one complained about seeing too little of the other.

"Oh my God," Grazyna repeats as she walks around. "This is going to be a big job."

But I soon hear *oohing* from another part of the room. She has come upon one of my mother's relics.

"Look at this lamp," she calls to me.

I don't have to look. I know the one she is talking about. It is a peach-colored dual scoop lamp with bendable stalks. Between the two tentacles, there are two faux cattails, made of brass dowel. My mother would not let me have this lamp.

"Oh wow," screams Grazyna from the dining room. "A starburst clock!"

I let Grazyna look around while I sit down in the living room. I feel strange and a little nauseous. The air is sharp with my mother's smells: ointment, liniment, disappointment. Mostly though, it stinks of her cigarettes, that nasty habit that seemed so glamorous, even healthful, if you read the advertisements of the times.

A black-and-white portable television rests on top of the old console color Motorola. I had been meaning to get my mother a new set. The TV Guide from two weeks ago is still tented on the ottoman. The fact that my mother left it that way makes me not want to move it, makes me think that she is just in the kitchen getting something to eat and will pop out any minute, bitching about something. The ottoman is an avocado Naugahyde number from the Seventies that is a tad too recent for my tastes, but I suppose the resale kids today would find it quite charming. Not I. It's hard to find the ridiculous relics of an era amusing, if you actively participated in that era.

Here, on this first night, I find myself studiously avoiding the basement. I can't explain why, but I feel afraid of it. So Grazyna and I explore the main floor of the house, snagging a few objects here and there, at Grazyna's insistence—the cattail lamp, the starburst clock, a sleek blue and white striped Sixties demitasse set, a wonderfully hideous swirl-glaze ashtray—making mental notes of what larger things to take later. Our peregrinations are interrupted only by my occasional fits of emotion. I cry for four or five minutes, Grazyna comforts me, then I'm fine until something else triggers another jag. When Grazyna pulled out a dusty cookbook of my mother's, the book opened to a recipe for "Zesty Swedish Meatballs." There was a small notation: "Jeff's favorite. Add extra tbsp. butter." I completely lost it. Grazyna was careful of what she showed me after that. But what can you do? A dead parent's home is full of emotional landmines, secreted in the terra firma of memory.

"Jeff, look at this," says Grazyna, as she digs through a cardboard box from the back of a cupboard. Inside there are dishes, a wonderful rare set of fifties Metlox Poppytrail with a very cool pattern: a multicolored rooster encircled by a wavy, dotty border. I didn't even know that my mother had these. Grief put aside for the moment, I drag the box over near the front door with the other items. We sort out some more things, things we don't like, and start to create a room: "Things to get rid of."

At the end of the night, we put the dishes and the other things into the car and scurry back to our tchotchke-filled postwar ranch house in an old but safe suburb. There, we make love, although in suggesting it, Grazyna does not phrase it in such a sensitive manner. She prefers the cruder, much more to the point, "I think we should fuck." So we do.

The next day, I tell Darrin, another art director at the agency, about the things we found at my mother's house. As I prattle on, his eyes widen exaggeratedly, a parody of listening. I soon realize that he's dying to get over there.

"So do you need any help?" he asks casually.

I try to keep from smiling. "No. I don't think so."

"You know, I've had some experience with estate sales. I know some people. I could help sort things out."

"No, I think we're going to handle everything ourselves," I say. I'm not entirely sure this is true, but it really doesn't matter. Just to make him crazy, I tell him about the set of Poppytrail dishes. It's fun to watch his face drop.

Grazyna and I can't get back over to the house until Wednesday night. I'm a little less emotional, but can't seem to put anything in the "To get rid of" room. It all seems to have too much value. I just can't figure out what *kind* of value, sentimental or ironic.

"Jeff, we *have* to get rid of some of this stuff," Grazyna reminds me, the slightest edge of annoyance in her voice.

I nod. "I know."

"We haven't even looked in the basement yet."

I exhale loudly, let my head drop. "I know. I don't even want to think about that until the weekend."

"Can we get rid of this?" she asks, holding up a cloth-covered fake wicker basket with an electrical cord trailing from it. She has found my mother's electric bun warmer. This is something Grazyna and I would never use, not even for laughs. In fact, it is the silliness of such items that usually allows me some perspective about the eras of which we are so fond. But in this case, the fact that my mother had an electric bun warmer breaks my heart. All the care she had once put into being a good little homemaker. I visualize the ad that lured her in: *Don't let your guests eat cold rolls!* I hear myself in response to Grazyna, "Let's just keep it for now."

Grazyna shakes her head, obviously humoring me. I feel bad for everything that goes into the "To get rid of" room. I also feel bad about the stuff that we keep: sleek black panther TV lamp, old dishcloths festooned with bouquets of flowers or bunches of fruit, a cookie jar shaped like a fat chef, a red and white Westclox kitchen clock, a Fiestaware teapot, a box of old Argosy magazines, set of brightly painted nested bowls. We find things that I had no idea my mother ever owned at all.

Grazyna volunteers to go through and bag up my mother's clothing for the shelter for abused women. She leaves me downstairs with orders to sort or else. Later, she comes down with two trash bags full of clothing for the shelter, but draped over her right arm are three or four of my mother's dresses from the early sixties (when she was about Grazyna's size), plus a beige car coat and a dress black coat with a fox collar. She finds nothing new in the "To get rid of" room. However, there are many new items in the pile to take home. Grazyna glares at me.

"I'm sorry," I say.

Grazyna shakes her head resignedly. She smiles and kisses me, tongue flickering warm into my mouth.

The next day at work, Darrin and two other people are in my office.

"How's the excavation going?" asks Darrin.

"Okay," I say, just finishing up a layout on my Mac. "We're uncovering a lot of stuff. Last night, I found one of those black panther TV lamps. It's even got the original bulb."

"Oh man, those are so cool," says Ellen, a copywriter.

I shrug. "I don't even remember it from when I grew up. My parents must have gotten sick of it and packed it away by the time I was born." I close up the file and quit InDesign. When I look up at my co-workers, I can practically see the envy in their eyes. They are thinking: *Gee, I wish my parents would hurry up and die.*

"I'll give you forty dollars for that lamp," Ellen says to me.

"No, sorry. Nothing's for sale. At least not right now." I open the program back up and frantically start adjusting the kerning on the type, just so I don't have to look at them.

They all leave my office dejected. I begin to regret that I said anything to anybody.

By late Friday night the house doesn't even look like the house anymore and it upsets me. Everywhere I look there are objects. Boxes, boxes, open cabinets and drawers, piles of things on top of other things. I can't breathe for all the things. I look for an empty chair so I can hyperventilate in relative comfort. Grazyna comes over to console me. She starts kissing me, which is kind of difficult when you're panting for breath, but between gasps, I find myself kissing back and before I know it, we are on the couch, flattening mounds of my mother's clothing, walled by boxes of my mother's things, dealing with my grief or whatever it is, in a rather unorthodox manner.

During it, Grazyna says to me, "You know, we really have to start on the basement."

"Grazyna, can't this wait?"

She rocks languidly above me. "It's just that you told me the basement was where all the really good stuff was."

"Grazyna," I say, cupping her breasts, those objects that I would never get rid of. "You sound like the people from work."

"If we ever want to get this behind us, we have to do it."

"All right. We'll do it tomorrow." Then, overcome by a rush of physical sensation, I forget about death: my mother's death, my wife's arousal by the objects of my mother's death, the taint of death in all irony, and I soar toward a small one of my own.

My mother put a lock on our basement door when she decided I was after everything she owned. I haven't been down in my parents' basement in at least ten years. Even back when my father was alive, this was our usual scenario:

"Mom? Can I go downstairs and look around? I want to see if you still have that wild orange lamp I remember from the old living room."

"Never you mind," she would say. "It's there and you're not getting your mitts on it until after I'm dead. Then you can have it all, but not before then."

Then my Dad would chime in. "Oh for Christ sakes, Dotty, let him have the lamp."

"No."

"But mom—"

"You heard me. Forget it."

And so it went. My mother was like that. If she didn't want you to do something, she meant it.

So early Saturday afternoon, after a Vietnamese lunch of Bun Bo Hue and Pho Ga on cardboard boxes, Grazyna and I break into my mother's basement. I grab a screwdriver from one of the kitchen junk drawers and shove it between the door and the jamb. With a crackle and a whiff of torn wood, the door creaks open. As I step down into the doorway, the air feels damper, heavier. I flick on the light switch. There is a flash of light, then a pop. We both flinch for a moment, then realize what it is. I head back into the kitchen for a flashlight and a new light bulb.

"I can't wait to see what's down there," Grazyna says to me from the basement doorway, as I search under the sink for bulbs.

I say nothing as I pluck a 75-watt bulb from behind a bottle of dish detergent.

We head down the stairs, flashlight on, to replace the bulb. The air is dank and fetid, how I would imagine a dungeon. Yet the walk down the stairs is eerily familiar, the feel of the banister against my hand, the creaks of the floorboards emboldened by age and moisture. I make it down to the bottom of the stairs and reach up to the socket. A long string hangs from the pull chain. The old bulb feels almost rusted into the socket, but I manage to unscrew it. New bulb in place, the foot of the stairs and the adjoining area are soon drenched with light.

The first thing I see is my parents' old living room set, a taupe couch and chair, chunky and pointy, arms like the rump of a '58 Mercury. A Danish modern coffee table, two matching end tables with a lamp on each, one orange, one pink. It is all streaked heavily with mildew. The chair is ragged with wear along the arms. The veneer on the tables is blotched and musty and bubbled from the swollen wood beneath. The lamps are in fair condition, but nowhere near as interesting as I remember. Part of me is amazed that it is all still here, while the other part of me is feeling a sickness again, the weight of objects.

"Yuck," says Grazyna, making a face. "What a mess."

"Yeah," I say. "I don't know what happened. They used to have a dehumidifier hooked up down here."

"It's here all right," she says, pointing to a rust-covered box on casters.

I take a strained breath of rank air. "Every once in a while, my mother would say 'I think we're going to call Purple Heart to come over to clean out the basement.' I know she said it just to scare me. Now I wish she had."

"What's this?" asks Grazyna, pointing to something pinned to the back of the couch. She unfastens a folded piece of paper with writing on it. "Jeff, I think it's a note." She peels it open. "Oh God, this is too weird. It's from your mother."

With two fingers, Grazyna proffers the note, which is rippled from dampness and mottled with small dots of mold.

Jeffrey—

I hope you're happy. You've finally gotten what you wanted—a chance to go down and loot the basement. Are you finding everything you've been wanting? Is it all as amusing as you hoped? I hope so. Now that your father and I are dead, you can finally redecorate.

Enjoy yourself,

Mother

Grazyna looks at me, incredulous. "That is so fucked-up," she says. "But it's *so* your mom."

I sit down on the couch.

"You all right?" asks Grazyna, resting her hand on my neck.

"Yeah, I guess." She watches me for a moment, then slowly walks over to the other side of the basement and turns on another light over a table with a lot of boxes on it. I can tell she can't seem to stop herself. Yet she's right about the note. This is so like my mother. It is so like her to take my fondness for the things of her time and twist it into some great affront. I don't even know what to say. I am too freaked to get mad or cry or anything.

"Wow," says Grazyna, yelling to me. "There's this great old canister set. And it's just ruined."

"Yeah," I say.

She looks under the newspapers at the table holding the boxes and yells to me. "I think it's a dinette set. Turquoise!" Then her voice drops with disappointment. "Yuk, these legs are totally messed up."

This is how it continues. Cool old stuff left to rot. I just let Grazyna go investigate everything. I look around me, at the living room furniture, all trashed, but arranged on the tattered rug just the way it was when I was growing up. There is a mound of my mother's cigarette butts in the big fish-shaped ashtray. She obviously came down here to smoke and drink and sit on the furniture she and my father owned when they were young. I'm sure she found it quite appropriate to sit on her own deteriorating furniture.

While Grazyna digs around on the other side of the basement, I lie back on the old couch, try to ignore the dust and must, and rest my eyes. I doze off to the sounds of rummaging: swollen cardboard boxes torn open; clink of chipped china; stomping of hundredth-generation silverfish; pained discoveries of a rusted past. I snooze fitfully, and can recall only fragments of dreams: I am out in the forest, a child on vacation with my mother and father at a place like Yellowstone Park. We are surrounded by endlessly tall moss-covered trees. When I walk through the trees by myself, I find topiary sculptures of chairs and tables and lamps. But they are black, and the ground is covered with their leaves. Nearby, my mother is throwing furniture in a big mound. I yell at her for scraping it all. Then I realize that I am under the pile of furniture. From beneath, I see a small stream of liquid bisect the air. It takes me a moment to realize that it's lighter fluid.

When I wake up, it's after five p.m. I have been sleeping for about three hours and feel well rested. There are streaks of mold on my shirt and pants. I stink of mildew, of rotting furniture, of the death of things. Grazyna is asleep next to me on a blanket from upstairs. There is a small pile of boxes next to the couch, all tagged with Grazyna's scrawl: "Vases and Planters (Shawnee)," "Xmas ornaments," "Chafing dish and Tom and Jerry set," "Bar Stuff." There are a few pieces of small furniture piled up, some of it in decent shape—an aluminum office chair, an end table, pink vinyl sewing bench ottoman and a few other things. I am too tired to even look at them.

I lean over and kiss Grazyna's forehead. She awakens and smiles at me. "Mmmm," she says, drowsily. "We should get this stuff home."

"You want to take this home?"

"Sure. Don't you?"

"It's getting so crowded there. Maybe we should give it away."

"Let's take it home."

I nod. "Yeah, okay."

We are done with my mother's house. We sold it to a broker for less than what my parents paid for the house in 1962. Trucks from the Purple Heart came and took away all the furniture, clothing, and appliances that we didn't want. What was ruined, we threw away. The rest of it—the kitsch, the pop, the hoke, the schlock—has landed here in our house. Our house has become a laughing shrine to a past I no longer understand. Everywhere I look in our living room, there is something old: Philco radio lamp, Chinese junk TV lamp, bowling ball liqueur dispenser, Haywood-Wakefield china cabinet. Sitting on our davenport that once felt so comfortable to me, paging through a Better Homes and Gardens decorating book from 1966 that Grazyna picked up at a garage sale, I feel like I am living on one of the pages: *Chapter 14: Redecorating makes your dreams come true!*

Grazyna is out of town visiting a friend in Grand Rapids this weekend. She deserved a weekend off, having worked harder than I did during all this.

"Are you going to be okay?" she asked me before she left.

"Of course. I'll be just dandy," I said.

But I'm not dandy. Somehow, all these things we own don't seem so wonderful to me anymore, as if I have been infected by the sincerity of the original owners. What about when I die? How will someone react to my things? I know the answer to that. I see it already when Grazyna and I are in some vintage resale shop cooing over some great winged midcentury monstrosity, then I look over and see some twenty-something slackers exchanging glances and stifled smiles. *Check out the geezers.* The thing is, they're buying stuff from the seventies and eighties. Just when does the statute of limitations on irony run out?

I pick up the phone and call Darrin. The phone rings twice. I worry that he isn't home, but he finally answers.

"Hello?"

"Darrin, it's Jeff," I say, no time for niceties. "We're having my estate sale. Right now, at my house." Before he says anything, I hang up. I make other calls, people at work, people I know from flea markets, vintage-store owners, anyone I can think of.

Within ten minutes, Darrin arrives. He's got his boyfriend Stefan with him. They have canvas bags and start filling them the moment they walk in. Five minutes later, more people arrive, then more. The vultures swarm:

"Oh my God, I love this piece!"

"Would you look at this?"

"The dishes! Where are the dishes?"

"Is that a *Thonet*?"

They come to me holding my treasures, the fruit of years of scavenging, then they go back for more. There is yelling, I hear breakage. It reminds me of the end of *The Day of the Locust*. I price everything as they bring it up to me; things are priced to move. Offers are made on the furniture, promises made to pick up later, scrawled SOLD signs taped on pieces, car trunks filled and bungee'd closed. People frantically drive back to borrow trucks.

That night, I am exhausted. I sit back on a couch, which no longer belongs to me, drink a beer, and happily survey my barren living room. The only things left in the house are the hand-me-down items we had when we first got married, the battered, the left over, the uncamp. Everything else, anything that anyone would want to display in their house, anything that anyone would want to snigger at or gush over, all that is gone. There were some things I did not, could not, sell, things that Grazyna brought to our marriage, from her normal life before me. Hopefully, she will forgive me all this, when she comes back to find her house emptied, a vessel of uncoolness. She will be furious at first, but I think she will eventually come to understand. Together we will start over. We will buy a beige plaid couch, an entertainment center, wall-to-wall carpeting, and we will be happy.

the problem with modell

unk is Modell's life. Modell owns a junk store. He tries to find things that look nice, but no one goes to his junk store to buy classy antiques, they go for bargains. When Modell tries to interest them in a piece of fine china or a good bentwood rocker, they ignore him. So Modell sticks to selling junk—old pots and pans, beat-up furniture, rusty tools—that sort of thing. Sometimes people bring the junk to him, which makes his job easy, but mostly he picks up the junk at people's houses.

Often, someone has just died, so Modell is forever picking through the dead people's things, the things the family no longer wants. Sometimes he will walk into a house and know that the person died just a couple of weeks ago. He can still smell the person. Not the smell of their dead body, just their smell. Their easy chair will still be pulled up close to the television. Sometimes there'll even be a snack on the TV tray next to the chair, a bowl of Cheetos or Pringles.

Modell himself has just suffered a loss. Kate, his sister. Kate was fifty-nine years old, a woman who lived alone all her adult life, except for the brief time she lived with Modell. This did not work out at all. It was five years before she and Modell spoke again. That was 1993. Once Modell made the first move to call her up, they started right back where they were before the big mistake. That is, Modell would go over to her house for dinner and she would tell him what was wrong with his life.

The problem with you, Modell, she would say, is that you're worried about everyone liking you. So they play you for a sap.

Last week, Modell put Kate in the ground. Afterward, he took the few people who showed up at the funeral for a little bite at the Big Boy's on Grand River. His treat. The next day, all Kate's stuff went into his store. Most of it was junk.

Today, Modell comes in early to clean up his shop. This is an almost impossible task because it is, well, a junk shop and there are things piled on top of other things then piled on top of stacks of more things. It's a big mess, but that's another thing people seem to want when they come into a junk shop. They like it when the place is disorganized, even a little filthy. It gives them the feeling that they will find something no one else has discovered. Which is absurd, because Modell has gone through it all again and again. He knows what everything is worth. He's seen the television shows. On the previous occasions where Modell has tidied and organized, people have complained. I liked it better the other way, they say. It was easier to find things that way.

Fine, Modell would say later in the truck, when he was alone. You want a big mess, I'll give you a big mess, goddamn it. The problem was, the place would get so messy sometimes, that it even got to Modell, who had pretty darned casual attitudes about clutter. But a bad mess in the store depressed him, gave him a bad self-image. As for this business of talking to himself in the truck: it is the only place where Modell tells people off. Modell is good at telling people off in the truck. He gives them a tongue-lashing, a good talking to; he reads them the riot act there in the truck. One time, when some customer tried to get him to come down too far on the price of an old CB radio, Modell really gave him hell later in the truck. Modell showed him no mercy in the truck.

Today, the reason Modell wants to get the store in shape is because someone is interested in buying it. Finally, Modell thinks, he has met someone who is a bigger sap than him. So after he changes into some decent clothes that he recently recovered from some corpse's closet, Modell tidies up the place as best he can—sweeping, stacking, organizing, discarding.

The place looks pretty good, if I do say so myself, Modell says to himself.

Later, at the appointed hour, the man doesn't show. Modell calls him, gets his answering machine, leaves a message. Modell suspects that the man has changed his mind. Maybe he is not such a sap after all, Modell thinks.

Because he has nothing better to do, Modell continues to clean the store, then flips the sign on the front door from WE'RE CLOSED to WE'RE OPEN. Almost immediately, someone comes in and buys an old coffee pot. Another person walks in, then walks out. This happens a lot. Sometimes they change their mind and get the hell out of there. Junk stores are not for everyone. Modell knows this. There are even some people who think they are better than Modell because he owns a junk store. This makes Modell mad, but he doesn't usually say anything. Maybe later, in the truck.

Imagine how Modell feels after he closes up the shop, the week after his sister dies, on the day he thinks he might be able to sell the whole kit and kaboodle, but doesn't, when he walks out to his parking lot and sees these words written in the dirt on the back window of his truck:

I Hate You Modell!

Why would someone write such a thing on Modell's truck? Sure, I can be a little grouchy sometimes, Modell thinks, as he smears the letters off with a rumpled tissue from his side pocket, but that's no reason to hate me. And with an exclamation point to boot! How could somebody be so mean?

It upsets Modell all the way home. How can you fight something like this? He feels helpless. He does not even know whom to tell off in the truck. Modell is distraught by the time he pulls into his driveway. The sight of his house does not really cheer him either. Today some neighborhood child has abandoned a Big Wheel in front of his porch. It may stay there for months.

Modell lives in an unglamorous part of Detroit, not that there are that many glamorous parts. Even though he's one of the few white folks around, the neighbors leave him alone, so Modell likes it okay. It's just that sometimes it depresses him. And today, seeing the Big Wheel on its side by his front porch, after someone has silently declared their hatred for him, just about nudges him to tears.

Later, in his living room, drinking a lukewarm can of Stroh's (fridge on the blink, house smells of sour milk), Modell still can't get those dusty words out of his mind. Could it have been one of the neighborhood kids? An irate customer? One of the people who bring him junk? Perhaps. Actually, the most likely suspect would be Kate, but she died. So who?

That night, as Modell tries to sleep, he goes through a list of people that might hate him with this kind of ferocity. The list isn't really that long, but if he goes back thirty-five years or so, he can get about a dozen solid names. Yet he couldn't help thinking, why would Tim Fleckerd from high school come by his store and write *I Hate You Modell!* on Modell's truck? Okay, so Modell did tell on him that time in Algebra class, junior year, for throwing an eraser, but he beat up Modell for that right after class, so that score was settled. Still, some wounds are deeper than others. Best not to rule Fleckerd out just yet.

Modell still can't get it out of his head that Kate has written the message.

It is impossible though. She had been in the hospital for weeks. Then just like that, she died. It was a surprise to everyone how quickly the cancer spread. Then the pneumonia. Still, though, maybe she has sent someone to do it for her. Or maybe he just didn't notice until today. Or she has come back from the dead just to make Modell miserable. If there was ever a reason for Kate to come back from the afterworld, that would be it. After a few hours of thrashing around in bed, Modell drops off to sleep.

The next morning, after three cups of Postum (How can you drink that swill? Kate would say. You must have rocks in your head.), Modell heads back to the store. He parks his truck in the gravel lot behind the place like he always does, but when he goes to unlock the back door, there is something written on it in chalk.

Modell Sucks!

Modell stands there for a moment, paralyzed. He looks around to see if anyone is watching him. He uses his shirtsleeve to wipe away the scrawling, then is sorry he does. Perhaps the police should be notified. These are, after all, like threats. Okay, not technically, but one can't be too careful. He opens the door and cautiously enters the store. Everything seems the same. The broom and dustpan are in the same place he left them. The cash register seems okay, but then he never leaves anything in it except a little change.

Modell sits down on the stool behind the cash register and thinks: Did they come by last night? Did they do it this morning? Modell thinks of the perpetrator in the collective evil plural, as is traditional in his west-side Detroit neighborhood. It is always *they* who break into a house or carjack someone or hold up a party store. *They* are very bad.

But I'm not bad, Modell says aloud. I'm really not. Talking to himself does not really help today. Modell gets up from the stool, walks over to the front door, unlocks it, and flips the sign to WE'RE OPEN.

The first person to come in is a regular who comes in every week, but never buys anything. Modell suspects him immediately.

Heard there was a death in your family, he says to Modell. Sorry to hear that.

How did you know that? says Modell, eyes narrowing at the regular.

Wasn't there a sign on your front door last week?

Oh, says Modell. Yes. My sister.

Sorry to hear that. The regular walks down one of Modell's aisles. Cleaned up, I see. Hard to find things now.

Fire inspector came by, told me I had to, Modell lies. Is he the one? Modell thinks he is.

Why do you hate me so? says Modell.

Pardon? says the regular.

You hate me. Why?

The regular puts down the hamburger press that he's been carrying around and says, I don't hate you, Modell. Whatever would give you that idea?

Oh you hate me all right. Don't deny it.

Modell, I don't hate you. I like you.

You do?

Yes I do. Really.

Well, I like you too.

The regular smiles at Modell, then walks down one of the rows, picks up an old record player that Modell has had for months, brings it over to the counter along with the hamburger press and gives Modell the asking price for both, no haggling.

No one else comes into the store all morning. Modell feels a little better after what happens with the regular. Modell is eating his usual lunch, a pressed turkey sandwich on white with mayo, when someone else comes in. (Why don't you eat something with some color in it? Kate would say. A little lettuce wouldn't kill you.) It is someone he has never seen before, a woman. She is immediately a suspect. Perhaps it is because she reminds Modell of Kate, albeit a younger version of her, with darker hair and a fuller bosom. Still, Modell can see the hate in her eyes. They are brimming with venom, he senses.

When she walks over to an old blue wheelbarrow filled with lamp parts, Modell believes she is planning something. Another one of her special messages perhaps. He looks around and wonders where it will wind up, maybe it has already been written, in charcoal on the sidewalk in front of the store or scratched into the paint of his truck. Or maybe she's come here to say what she really thinks of Modell right to Modell's face. That's probably it—Modell sees himself afterward, utterly deflated. Modell decides to be very nice to her so she'll have mercy on him.

Can I help you?

She smiles at Modell, a kind smile. Here it comes, thinks Modell.

No, I'm just looking, thanks.

There is nothing to do but pray she'll go easy on me, thinks Modell. Let me know if there's anything I can help with, he says.

All right.

Have I done anything to offend you?

Heavens no. What makes you say that? You've got a nice little store here. Glad I found it.

Oh.

Is it possible that she isn't the one? No. Modell has a feeling. It's still coming. This being nice is simply to throw him off. But when she comes up to the counter with an old washing machine motor and a beat-up toaster oven, she smiles again at Modell, pays her money and leaves. In a moment, all that is left of her is the sound of the bell as she passes back through Modell's front door.

This process of spotting the message writer is repeated a dozen times throughout the afternoon. Each time, Modell is certain that person is the one who hates his guts. Each time, it's not the person.

As far as he knows.

But for some reason, with all the questions he asks everybody, it seems like there is much more activity in the store than usual. People keep telling him that no, they really like him. It gets to the point where Modell actually starts to believe a few of them. Also, people buy much more than they usually buy. Though Modell suspects that they will never again return.

At the end of the business day, Modell has made a decent amount of money. He sweeps up and locks the front door. He takes a final walk through the store, looking for a new message. He is both scared and excited. He examines the back door when he leaves, but he finds nothing. The same with his truck. No new messages anywhere.

He goes home, prepares a dinner of wieners sliced into a pot of baked beans, watches a little television. All evening, a feeling of vague disappointment nags at him. For a while, before Modell goes to sleep, he thinks that Kate would have been good to talk to about this, but then remembers that if she were alive, she would be one of the main suspects.

The next morning when he pulls up behind the store though, he sees that whoever it is has been busy again. On the back door and the brick that surrounds it, someone has spray-painted in red:

Die Modell Die!

There are a few swastikas here and there as well, which is strange because Modell is not Jewish. He doesn't even know any Jews. Well, he probably does, he just does not realize it. For some reason, Modell is not as alarmed at this as he was by the others. In fact, he decides not to call the police and sets about scrubbing it off his door and bricks. It comes off surprisingly easy. Afterward, Modell has the sense of a job well done. He will find this person or persons, then—well, he's not sure what he'll do, but he'll do something.

As the day progresses, Modell's calmness about the whole thing bleeds back into panic and he again questions his customers:

Why would you do such a thing?

Do you have hatred for me in your heart?

If you harm me, I'll have no choice but to contact the authorities.

The customers are not as amused today as they were the day before. Some are offended after Modell speaks to them, others walk out in a huff, the rest, they just think Modell is a little nuts, which they have thought all along.

The few who find it charming are the ones who truly believe in the essential good of the junk shop. They believe the junk shop is a necessary function, an important part of the economic system. They also believe that in order for the junk shop to properly flourish, it must have a quaint eccentric at the helm. To them, Modell is just this. So one of them chuckles and replies that she understands and that she has learned her lesson. Modell seems satisfied at this.

So when he flips his sign, locks up the store for the day, and walks out to the parking lot to find the windshield of his truck smashed in with a cinderblock, Modell does not know what to do. At first he is mad, then confused, then sad. Someone really does hate me, thinks Modell, and it's probably not that nice lady. They are going to kill me and there's nothing I can do about it. He brushes the glittering bits of safety glass off his front seat and dashboard, pulls out the remains of the windshield and throws it onto the gravel behind his store. He then puts on his sunglasses and drives home.

But they don't kill him. Expecting them to come during the night and finish the job, Modell is surprised when nothing happens. After a night of fitful sleep waiting for death's messenger to come take him, Modell wakes to an overcast, yet bright gray morning. He skips breakfast, in a hurry to get to the shop and get this all over with, not making any preparations, knowing that everything with his estate will basically take care of itself. Tor, his quiet nephew, has been named in his will. He leaves instructions for Sammy, a fellow junk shop owner, to take over the store, sell everything he can at rock-bottom prices. The junk store vultures will handle the rest.

Yet, that day at the store, it is quiet. There are no new threats etched into the surface of his life. Modell expecting death with every customer, but making only sales, and quite a few of them at that. The day passes without incident.

That week, as he awaits his grisly demise, business is great. By Thursday, Modell realizes that he is having his best week in the history of the store, having moved all sorts of junk at excellent prices.

On Friday, the man who had wanted to purchase Modell's store comes in unexpectedly and asks Modell if he still wants to sell.

Modell says he'll need to think about it.

east side

how could there be so many wig shops in one city?

In all the shopping districts in Detroit where there were once swanky department stores, then nothing, there were now wig shops.

They must somehow materialize spontaneously, he thought as he walked, like urban renewal colors—electric blues, lemon yellows, titty pinks—abruptly slathered on the cinder-block facades of Chaldean party stores. Still, those colors were there to brighten and mollify and distract.

But wig shops?

He stopped in front of one of the places: Lovely Wigs, Inc. The sign was in coarse, hand-lettered script. Two uneasy rows of wigs ran the length of the display window, staggered above and below eye level. They were set on slick, bald, brown-and-cream-colored heads. Heads with sanded-down ears and faces, empty hints of eyes, faint mouths bent into numb smiles. Some of the heads had stunted or elongated throats, some were cut right at the neck, while taller ones from the top row were taken at the collarbone.

The heads meant nothing. They were there only to hold up the wigs, to show off the many styles and colors: burnt-blond; short, curly auburn; platinum blond; long, straight dark; plus a mammoth silvery wig that towered over the others, with dark and light intertwined, sprawling and conflicting, a city block of hair, the kind of hair that could take over a neighborhood, but never did.

He paced the sidewalk in front of the window; eyes only on the wigs, letting them weave all into each other, liking the effect, when an old woman came out of the wig shop.

She looked at him. He looked at her head, at the dark nest atop it. The old woman preened a little for him. She was proud of her wig.

Part 2

"That's a lovely wig," he said, tipping his head to indicate the wig.

"You're not supposed to say that," said the old woman, lips flattened against her false teeth. She stormed off down the street.

"I'm sorry," he said.

He looked at his reflection in the window of the wig shop. He kept looking, then shifted his body a little. He moved his head with precise adjustments, secretly aligning his image beneath one of the wigs, a high goldish hat of curls. Because he was leaning down and over from where he stood, he could only keep his head in the correct position for about forty seconds before his calf cramped.

He tried another wig, a dark mid-length. He actually had to shift his feet and entire body this time, twisting his hips until the wig fit. He admired himself and went on to the next one.

Without knowing it, a small crowd started to form around him, the people watching him make the oblique movements, not knowing that he was carefully placing each wig on his own reflection. Soon there were seven or eight people watching. When they realized what he was doing, they too tried to move their bodies so their likenesses fit just beneath the wigs. A few more people gathered.

By then, he was quite absorbed, delicately touching the air above his head with open hands, sometimes poking, other times smoothing. The wigs were looking good on a real face.

Finally, he noticed what was happening around him: people crowding at the window, trying on the various wigs, silently moving their bodies, superimposing their faces beneath the wigs. Soon, there were not enough to go around, so he stepped back from the window. Someone immediately took his place beneath the giant silver wig. He stood there, watching the people glide between each other, never really touching, but keeping close in the small space of the window.

hearts and bones

*All knowledge, the totality of all questions and answers,
is contained in the dog.*

Franz Kafka

five months of marriage and still when Walker strolled unannounced into the room where Megan read, all this happened in a moment: She would look up at him, alarmed at first, then bewildered, as if to say, "What the fuck are you doing here?" Then abruptly, it seemed to Walker, she would remember and try quickly to smile. Her worst, most obviously fake smile—a grimace, a death mask, you name it.

That smile was what made Walker one day suddenly suggest a drive. A long drive to Mandrake, Michigan. They could visit his grandparents there for a few hours, but mostly they would drive and talk and spend time together, get used to each other in this new way.

"Just for the day," said Walker. "It'll be fun. We'll see each other, we'll see my grandparents. It'll be nice."

Megan was not thrilled. Walker was full of these kinds of ideas. She had never met his grandparents (a slight fall had kept them from the wedding), and was frankly not all that anxious to meet them. Her dealings with grandparents had been spotty at best. Her favorite grandfather, who drank rye whiskey neat, smelled of Tiparillos, and taught her how to shoot craps, died when she was twelve years old. Her one remaining grandmother (Czech, on her mother's side), tried constantly to force all of her ancient opinions on Megan, along with extraordinarily dry Eastern European pastries that instantly absorbed all the saliva in Megan's mouth, thus rendering her silent. This, she assumed, was her grandmother's reason for serving them. If she was lucky, Megan only had to see this grandmother two or three times a year.

"Couldn't we just go for an aimless drive somewhere?" said Megan. "We could check out that big wheel of cheese over in Ohio. It's supposed to be the world's largest."

"Come on. I haven't seen my grandparents in ages. I know they'd like to meet you."

Megan agreed to go. It was more to appease Walker than anything else.

They left early the following Saturday. It was about a four-hour drive from Ferndale (an old town just along the rim of Detroit) to Mandrake. Megan read most of the way, a Dawn Powell novel, *The Happy Island.* After a few tries, Walker gave up on the idea of sharing meaningful conversation and amused himself by listening to the polka and country music stations that faded in and out on the AM radio.

Not long after they passed a bleached city limits sign barnacled with Rotary, VFW, and Optimists emblems, Walker pulled the car into the driveway of a brilliantly groomed green and white bungalow. A small cedar sign on the lamppost read in carved script: *The Stanhopes.*

Walker opened the door of the car and waited for Megan to do the same. "Come on, let's go," he said.

"Do I have to?" asked Megan, looking up from her book.

"You can't stay in the car."

"Sure I can. I have water. And snacks." Megan held up a bag of Combos to prove it. Then she looked across the lawn and saw a small elderly couple watching and waving to her from behind a picture window. Resigning herself, she exhaled loudly, dropped the bag, and opened the car door. By the time she and Walker approached the front porch, the couple was at the door, waiting for them.

The man and woman were both well into their seventies, both as immaculate as the corners of the front lawn. Mrs. Stanhope was wiping her hands with a flowered dishcloth when she greeted them. Megan thought she looked like a TV grandmother except for the long pink cigarette that dangled from the edge of her mouth. Mr. Stanhope stood slightly behind her, his hand on the left side of his wife's waist, fingers resting along the top of the curve of her buttock. Their frail sloped torsos were touching, squeezed together was how it looked to Megan.

Walker greeted them excitedly. He rushed forward and hugged his grandparents both at the same time. Then he stepped back and introduced Megan.

"Hi," she said, holding her hand up. She then gave them both quick, perfunctory embraces. They all just stood for a moment, smiling. Megan's smile was frozen into place. Then Mr. Stanhope cocked his head and looked at Megan as if he were deciding something.

"You have a lovely home," said Megan, to divert his attention and break the silence. She looked around at all the lace and knickknacks that seemed to her to be standard issue for the homes of old people. Then she focused on a large mounted alligator head with a Farm & Fleet hat on it. Walker and his grandmother started talking about someone she did not know—an Aunt Stella. Megan couldn't think of anything else to say.

"Thanks," said Mr. Stanhope, directly addressing her. "We're very happy here, the three of us."

"There's someone else?"

Mr. Stanhope nodded. "Come on, I'll give you the four-bit tour." He turned to his wife and Walker, who were by that time laughing about Aunt Stella threatening someone with her colostomy bag. "Marilyn, I'm going to show Megan around. Why don't you two make us some ice tea?"

Walker and his grandmother stopped laughing and looked at each other. Walker raised his eyebrows coyly. "You do that, El. We'll get tea," said Mrs. Stanhope. She and Walker turned around and headed toward the kitchen. There was more laughing. Megan watched the two of them, wanting to follow.

"You want to see the kitchen?" asked Mr. Stanhope. "We might as well start the tour there. Come on."

As they neared the kitchen doorway, Megan could see Walker getting a small box of tea bags from the middle shelf of a red and white cupboard. Mrs. Stanhope was standing next to him. She turned right around when Megan and Mr. Stanhope walked in.

"I thought you two would be back," she said. "Elvin, I have something for you." She opened a cupboard door, reached in, and grabbed something. She pressed it into her husband's hand. Megan could not see what it was.

"Thank you, dear." Mr. Stanhope put it in his left shirt pocket. "I'll keep it right here." He made an *X* with his finger on the unbuttoned flap of the pocket.

Christ. These people were really something, thought Megan. She hoped this wouldn't take too long.

"Well, you've seen the kitchen. Pretty exciting, huh?" said Mr. Stanhope. "Let's move on."

She tried to smile. Why did midwesterners always have to give you a tour of their house?

Mr. Stanhope went through the rooms briskly, not pointing out details. Megan, satisfied that she didn't have to talk, let it all breeze by, a blur of musty cottage smells and soft, heavily laundered colors. They ended the tour in a screened porch at the back of the house. The floor was covered with blue Astroturf that crackled beneath Megan's feet. Two ornate wrought iron patio chairs stood about a foot and a half apart. Between them was a small dog, a brown and white beagle, a little gray around the maw. The dog sat there placidly, the link between the two chairs.

"Let's rest a bit here and wait for our tea," said Mr. Stanhope.

Before Megan could sit down, Mr. Stanhope knelt down in front of the dog. Megan heard his knees crack in quick succession, one right after the other. Standing there, she could see dark areas on the old man's bald head, like tiny unknown countries on a globe. She noticed that he was wearing a flannel shirt, though it was late summer in Michigan.

The dog got up, walked a few steps closer to him, and then sat again. Mr. Stanhope cradled the dog's head in his mottled hands and addressed it: "Hello, Princess. Hello. Princess, show us how smart you are."

At this point, it was no surprise to Megan that the dog was named Princess. Of course it was.

He reached into his shirt pocket. Whatever had been there was now closed in his palm. He gave the dog a peek at it. Princess growled. Mr. Stanhope's eyes widened. Megan wondered what the hell was going on.

"Okay, Princess."

"Grrrr," said the dog.

"Come on, girl." Another peek.

"Grrrrrrr."

"All right. Get ready, Princess."

"Grrrrrrrrr."

He showed the dog the bone-shaped biscuit in his hand. "Who's this from?"

"Grrrrraaammmmma."

The dog spoke.

Megan could not believe it. She had no idea what was going to happen, and then *the fucking dog spoke*. The word was still floating in front of her. *Grandma*. Impossible. It was too weird. No, it was possible, just the result of practice, a lot of time spent by a sweet, bored old man, a labor of love. Still, though. *Grandma*. Megan didn't know why, but it seemed like one of the most incredible things she had ever witnessed.

Mr. Stanhope looked over at Megan, who was obviously stunned. "Nice going," he said to the dog. Princess held out her paw. Mr. Stanhope shook it, then held the dog's head close to his and kissed her pointy nose. The dog yowled gently.

Walker and his grandmother entered the back porch. Mrs. Stanhope was carrying a TV tray with four filled glasses. Walker had two folding chairs. Megan turned to Walker, but couldn't say anything. She just gestured toward the dog and then started laughing.

"I see you got the show," said Walker, grinning as he set up the chairs. "Pretty wild, huh?"

Megan watched the dog run out the back door, off toward a small tidy garden bordered by low loops of white wire fencing. Then she was finally able to speak. "Mrs. Stanhope, your dog and your husband are amazing. I've never seen anything like that. They should go on television."

Mrs. Stanhope smiled. "Yes, El is very talented. That's why I married him." She looked over at her husband.

Mr. Stanhope waggled his eyebrows, mock lecherous.

Megan had not seen old people carry on in this way. She wasn't sure how she felt about it.

"Anyway, I don't do anything," said Mr. Stanhope. "Princess does it all. Speaking of which—" He stood up when he saw the dog carrying something in its mouth from the garden. "Goddamn it, Princess, put that back!" he yelled. "Crazy dog digs up all our tulip bulbs then eats the damn things. Or buries them like they were bones."

"Come on, let's sit down and have our tea," said Mrs. Stanhope.

On the way home that afternoon, it became obvious to Walker that the trip to Mandrake had made an impression on Megan. She could not stop talking about the dog—how smart it was, how she had never seen anything so strange and funny. There were also questions about his grandparents—how long had they been married, what were they like when they were younger, things like that. Walker was surprised to see her so enthusiastic. It was kind of fun.

"You really think the dog is amazing, don't you?" he said to Megan.

"Yes I do. Don't you?"

"It's a good trick."

"Trick? That was amazing. It's more like a miracle."

"Oh, come on." Walker chuckled, held one palm up, and raised his voice to a priestly Irish brogue. "Ahh, The Miracle of the Talking Dog."

"Shut up, Walker."

Megan actually seemed hurt. "I'm sorry," he said. But it *was* silly, because he had been watching that trick for the past eight or nine years. Still, he had never seen Megan get that way about anything.

"How long have they had Princess?" asked Megan.

"I think about eleven years. My grandpa brought her home as a pup. A gift for my grandmother."

"Really?"

"They used to take her everywhere. When I was still living at home, they didn't live very far away and sometimes in the evenings they'd walk over to our house with the dog and they would both hold the leash. I remember thinking it was pretty goofy."

Megan just nodded. She was lost in dog thought.

During the week that followed, Walker startled Megan only once, while she was reading a book of urban folklore called *The Choking Doberman.* She said some of the legends were sort of creepy and that's why he had scared her when he walked into the room. But even though her smile was not as stiff as usual, Walker still saw that realization flash across her face. *Oh yeah, he lives here.*

Saturday, Walker decided to surprise Megan with lunch. He walked into the living room carrying a tray with two grilled cheese sandwiches and two mugs of cream of tomato soup on it. Megan looked up, unsuspecting, and started laughing when she saw the sandwiches.

"I haven't had this sort of lunch since I was twelve years old," she said.

Walker handed her a plate and put the mugs on the floor. "I thought you might enjoy it."

"Thanks, but shouldn't we be watching cartoons or something?"

Walker laughed. "Just eat the fucking sandwich, smartass."

"Now that *really* reminds me of my childhood." She took a bite.

It was the first thing Megan had eaten all day and she hadn't realized how hungry she was. She and Walker sat on the couch and ate the sandwiches, their plates balanced precariously on joined knees, their chewing interrupted only by occasional sips of soup. They did not say anything for at least five minutes.

Megan finished the sandwich. Her fingers were oily, covered with tiny crumbs. She pulled a tissue from her T-shirt pocket (Walker always forgot the napkins) and pressed it to the pads of her fingers. She looked up and saw Walker watching her, smiling. It embarrassed her a little.

"I talked to my mother last night," she said.

"How's she doing?" said Walker, licking a thumb.

"Fine. She and dad are going camping up north for a few days." She put the tissue back in her pocket.

"When?"

"Thursday. They asked if I would stay at their house while they were gone."

"Oh, boy. More house-sitting," said Walker, dryly. He would be spending another lovely weekend at home alone. "Okay, whatever. When are you going over there?"

"Thursday night."

"Okay," Walker gathered the plates and stood.

"Look, why don't you take the day off too, and come along?"

"You mean stay at your parents' house with you?"

"Why not?" Megan got up from the couch and kissed him. "It'll be fun. We'll have wild suburban sex. Do it in a McMansion. We'll defile something beige."

When Walker's mother called three weeks later, Walker and Megan were in Chicago, visiting some friends. Megan had felt like getting out of town for a few days. Walker answered his cell phone and when the voice on the line said, "It's about Grandma," he immediately thought of "The Miracle of the Talking Dog." He smiled and tried not to listen to what his mother was saying.

It didn't work. He couldn't keep from hearing that his grandmother had had a stroke the day before and had died. "She was weeding in her garden," his mother said. She talked about the arrangements. As he listened, Megan walked over and sat next to him. She could tell that something was wrong.

When Walker finally spoke, he said that he and Megan would drive up for the funeral. His mother thought it would be better if they didn't. There were already too many people. Grandpa just wanted to be left alone. "Stay and finish your trip," she said. "Everything has already happened."

After he hung up, Megan put her arms around him.

As soon as Walker and Megan got home from Chicago, they planned to go to Mandrake. They made plans for the following four weekends. Each time, they couldn't make it. Work, or some unavoidable commitment.

Walker called his grandfather a few times, but they never talked for long. He usually sounded tired and not terribly enthusiastic about company. Walker certainly didn't blame him, but it was after they spoke that he wanted most to visit. Megan wanted to go too, even though she didn't think it would be good to ask to hear the dog talk again.

Walker's parents drove up to Mandrake about every other weekend. It was how Walker got most of the progress reports on his grandfather. ("He seems lonely," Walker's father would say. "But he doesn't seem to want to be with us.")

At Christmas, Walker spoke to his grandfather on the phone for at least a half hour, and afterward he and Megan once again made up their minds to visit. But the winter weather was unpredictable, and it made planning a car trip almost impossible.

Spring broke unseasonably early. One night in April, while Walker's parents were in Mandrake, seven months and twenty-three days after Walker and Megan's visit, during the dinner that Walker's mother had prepared, his grandfather quietly excused himself from the table to go lie down. He gave both his son and daughter-in-law a light kiss on the forehead before turning in. Although he had never done that before, neither of them thought it strange at the time.

Walker's father found the body in bed an hour and a half later. ("It was the best he'd looked in a long time," Walker's father said on the phone.) A local doctor had told them, "These sorts of successive deaths were not uncommon among elderly couples."

The day before the funeral, Walker and Megan arrived in Mandrake and went directly to the house. There was no answer at the door, so Walker used the spare keys he had brought from his parents' place.

The house was quiet. The small sounds they made while entering seemed almost absorbed by the silence: door opening; keys on table; tile click of suitcase. Everything looked exactly as it had when he and Megan were last there.

"What do we do now?" said Megan.

"My folks must have gone to the store or something. I'm sure they won't be long." Walker lowered himself onto the couch in the living room, picked up a magazine to keep his mind off everything. It was a copy of *Modern Maturity*.

Megan didn't feel like sitting down. She walked over to the hallway to look at photographs on the wall. Her eye was immediately drawn to a picture of her and Walker, one that she hated, taken shortly after they were married. There were other pictures too, Walker as a child, his family, cousins, uncles, aunts. Megan searched around and found Walker's grandparents' wedding picture. It looked a lot like other wedding pictures she had seen from the thirties and forties, but what was odd were the expressions on their faces. Mr. and Mrs. Stanhope, looking like dressed-up kids, staring stiffly at the camera, barely smiling, not at all the happy couple she had met. They seemed uncomfortable; hands curled downward like the gawky poses of immigrants, balanced unsteadily on strange and foreign terrain.

There was a bark from the backyard. Megan turned and looked at Walker.

"I was wondering why you didn't ask," he said.

"I thought maybe it might bother you," said Megan.

"I don't think so."

Megan walked over and sat next to Walker. "What's going to happen to her?"

Walker tossed the magazine onto the end table. "I don't know. My parents can't keep her. My mom doesn't really like dogs."

"Your grandparents were really crazy about her, weren't they?"

"I suppose they weren't the only ones," he said. Megan did not acknowledge his attempt at humor.

"When did he teach her, you know, the thing?" Megan stammered, then looked away from Walker.

"I think about a year or so after he got her." Walker tried to keep from smiling. For some reason, this was making him feel better. "Any other questions?"

"It's not funny, Walker."

"I guess not. Come on."

"Where?"

"Just come on."

As soon as they walked into the backyard, they noticed the tulips blooming in the middle of the lawn. There were not a lot of them, just three or four, swaying in the grass like tall, gaudy weeds. Walker was bewildered at first—neither of his grandparents would ever plant them that way. Then Megan remembered how Princess liked the taste of the bulbs, how she liked to bury them.

The dog ran right up to Megan. Princess, who looked about the same, perhaps a little grayer, completely ignored Walker. He was used to this. Dogs and cats, given a choice, always selected Megan, as if she held some honorary degree from the animal kingdom. The dog put her front paws up on Megan's legs. Walker watched as his wife knelt, cupped her hands around Princess's head, and ran her fingers through her fur.

He watched the two of them playing and listened to the wind shiver the trees that surrounded the backyard. The leaves were still new, and the wind flashed through one tree, then the next and next and on, creating an oval of shuddery white sound that seemed to enclose the three of them. He felt something rushing inside him, making the same sound, as he watched Megan. She was stroking the dog's head and sides, she was cooing to it. "Hello, Princess. What a good dog. *Hello. Hello. Hello.*"

Seeing them together, Walker felt sure the dog recognized Megan from the one visit. Princess rolled over onto her back.

"Want me to rub a tummy? Do you like that? Hmmm?" Megan saw Walker watching her and suddenly blushed. "She *is* a sweet dog." Princess's leg was twitching.

"Want me to get the biscuits?" asked Walker.

Megan nodded eagerly.

Walker returned to the backyard with a shirt pocket full of Milk-Bones. He secretly handed one to Megan, so the dog wouldn't see. "You try," he said. "I assume you remember."

"Have you ever done it?" asked Megan.

"My grandpa was the only one who could get her to talk. I really wouldn't get your hopes up."

Megan spoke to the dog again. "Come on, Princess. Sit up." Megan patted her when she rose. "Good girl."

"Now show her the Milk-Bone real quick," said Walker. "Just a peek."

Megan did just that. "See it?"

The dog growled.

"That's good," said Walker.

"Grrrrr."

"Okay, Princess," said Megan. The biscuit was tight in her hand.

"Grrrrrrr."

"Get ready, girl."

"Grrrrrrrr."

"Now show her the biscuit," said Walker, excited.

"Come on, Princess." She revealed the Milk-Bone. "Who's this from?"

The dog barked and started begging frantically. After a moment, Megan gave her the biscuit.

"I think she's forgotten," said Walker.

"I don't think so," said Megan. "I'll just have to learn how."

After two more tries, Megan gave the dog a hug, then she and Walker went back into the house for something cold to drink while they waited for Walker's parents to return.

Because it was stuffy in the house, Walker and Megan brought their drinks out on the back porch. They sat on the two wrought iron chairs, talking animatedly about anything, forgetting for the moment what had brought them there. Megan said something that made Walker start laughing. Something about mowing the flowers. As he laughed, she reached up, put her hand on the back of Walker's head. The dog, seeing two people on the porch, scratched at the screen door, waiting to be let in.

mystery spot

We are tourists.

I have recently come to terms with this. My husband and I were never the kind who traveled to expand our minds. We always traveled to have fun—Weeki Wachee, Gatlinburg, South of the Border, Lake George, Rock City. We have seen swimming pigs and horses, a Russian palace covered with corn, young girls underwater drinking Pepsi-Cola from the seven-ounce bottle, an automobile tire over six stories tall, a cycling cockatoo riding a tightrope.

I guess we always knew.

This, our last trip, was appropriately planned at the last minute, the luxury of the retiree. It is one that I'm glad I decided we take, although everybody (doctors, friends, children) forbade us to go. "I strongly, strongly advise against this, Ella," said one of my seemingly hundreds of physicians. But we needed a trip, more than we've ever needed one. Besides, the doctors only want me to stay around so they can run their tests on me, poke me with their icy instruments, spot shadows inside of me. And they have already done plenty of that.

I decided to take action. Our van was packed and ready. We have kept it that way ever since retirement. So I kidnapped my husband John and we headed for Disneyland. This is where we took our kids, so we like it better than the other one. Besides, at this point in our lives, we are more like children than ever. Especially John.

It is a lovely trip so far, quiet and steady. The miles are moving no faster than they should be, which is fine with me. When I see the sign, we are just about out of Nebraska and into some hillier terrain. It is along the rolling side of the interstate, a gaudy orange and yellow billboard, the kind that would have driven Lady Bird Johnson crazy, what with all her plans to beautify America.

VISIT THE AMAZING
"MYSTERY SPOT!"
43 miles

Amazing, indeed. I decide we should give it a try. On this trip, if something looks like fun, we stop. No more traveling in a hurry for us. There were too many vacations like that with the kids. Three days to get to Florida, four to California—*we've only got two weeks*—rush, rush, rush. Now there's all the time in the world. Except I'm falling apart and John can barely remember his name. That's all right. I remember it. Between the two of us, we are one whole person.

YOU CAN'T MISS IT
THE BAFFLING "MYSTERY SPOT"
20 miles

There are a lot of signs leading to this place. I watch for them and count them down like the kids used to do with the signs for Stuckey's. Every day on the road, traveling with Kevin and Cindy, we'd encounter at least one of those crazy places with their pecan logs and tepid coffee. Sometimes the signs would start a hundred miles away. Then there would be a new one every ten, fifteen miles. The kids would get all worked up and want to stop and John would say no, we had to get some miles under our belt. The kids would beg and beg, and finally, when we were a half-mile away, he'd give in. The kids would scream *yay* and John and I would look at each other and smile like parents who knew how to spoil their children just enough.

"Remember Stuckey's, John? I haven't seen one of those places in years," I say.

"Oh yeah," he says, nodding, staring blankly at the road. But he doesn't remember. This is something we have both gotten used to. Every once in a while, he knows enough to realize that he has forgotten everything, but these moments happen less and less these days. It doesn't matter. I am the keeper of the memories. It has been that way for quite some time. With John's mind, first the corners of the blackboard were slowly erased, then the edges, and the edges of edges, creating a circle that grew smaller, smaller, before finally disappearing into itself. What is left are only smudges of recollection here and there, places where the eraser did not completely do its job, memories that I hear again and again. It is surprising how well he still drives though. After all our car trips in the past, I don't think he'll ever forget how. And now, as the physical part of our person, it is one of his official duties. Anyway, once you get into the rhythm of long-distance driving, it is only a matter of direction (my job as well, mistress of the maps), avoiding those sudden, unexpected exits, and looking out for the danger that comes up fast in your mirror.

SEE FOR YOURSELF!

THE INCREDIBLE "MYSTERY SPOT"
This Exit

We get off the freeway and follow another car, a blue one, with its rear wheels riding way over to the left. "That man's car is so out of alignment, it looks like he's trying to pass himself," I say to John. He does not answer. After a half-mile or so, we end up in a huge gravel parking lot with about four or five other cars. There is a sign, brash and bright, like all the others:

"MYSTERY SPOT"
IT'S RIGHT HERE!

I'm glad to get here. My knees feel swollen and stiff. I need to stretch them and get myself to a bathroom on the double. After John parks the van, I grab my good four-pronged aluminum cane and we head on in.

After we both use the can, I go get our tickets ($6.50!). We then head outside, where there is a little shuttle bus idling, ready to take us to the Mystery Spot. I'm hoping there won't be too much walking after that, but I won't let it stop me. Not this trip. Inside the bus, there is already a family of four (they have a son and a daughter, just like us), plus one man by himself. The single man is wearing a silly foreign sailor hat, a shrunken blue T-shirt, and big shorts with Budweiser beer emblems all over them. Slouched there, with his pale arms crossed, he looks like a big thirty-five-year-old child. Luckily, he sits in the back, near the family. John and I are behind the driver, a young shy-looking black man. In front of him, on the dashboard, is a yellow stick-on note.

"I feel great & ready!"
YES-YES-YES

I wonder what he's ready for. I hope it's to drive safely. The young man puts the bus into gear, but before we take off, he gets on the PA. Reading from a script, he says, "Hello and welcome to the Mystery Spot. It will be about a ten-minute ride to the area with the mysterious powers. So sit back and prepare to be amazed."

"He has a nice speaking voice," I whisper to John. He grunts, the way he's always grunted. This is one thing he has not forgotten, unfortunately. I shift around, try to get comfortable in my cramped seat. Finally, I give up and just read the brochure they gave us:

At "Mystery Spot," you'll see many astonishing things that seem to defy the laws of nature, yet are simply natural illusions. It is a place where gravity seems to have disappeared, where your sense of balance seems entirely upset. Everything you know turns upside down and you are pulled in directions that never before seemed possible. It's entertaining for young and old alike!

"The key word here is 'seems,'" I say to John. He says nothing, points out the window at the Mammoth Gift Shop passing by. John is well trained after years of spotting gift shops for me on the road. At one time, that was my favorite part of vacation, the bringing back of things. My personal weakness was pottery. No matter where we traveled, I always came back with a little something—Indian pots from Wyoming and Montana, beautiful glazed vases from Pigeon Forge, Mexican bowls from the southwest. All beautiful, and most of it still packed away in boxes in our basement. A home, after all, only has so much room. These days, there might be a trinket or two brought back for the grandchildren, but we are done with all that. To possess things, you need time.

All those boxes. The kids are going to have quite a job ahead of them.

I peek behind us. The man in the Budweiser shorts is talking to the family. You can tell that the husband and wife are a little put off by him. The kids seem to like him though. I'm surprised he isn't talking to us. He looks crazy, and crazy people love old people. We're just good targets. Probably because we can't get away as quickly. In the past ten years or so, whenever John and I have been in a city, it isn't long before we're approached by bums, bunko artists, or just plain kooks.

"Glad he's sitting in the back," I whisper. I notice that John is taking a little nap. I let him rest. Driving is hard work. After a few minutes, the shuttle bus stops. We pull up by a bench at the edge of a field surrounded by trees.

The kids are the first out, the mother and father right behind them. I wake John up and have him give me a hand because my knees have stiffened up again. I try to keep myself from cursing as I get up. To top it off, the Budweiser man is waiting for us to get off the bus. We just ignore him and head for the asphalt path that leads through the trees.

THIS WAY TO
"MYSTERY SPOT"

Halfway into the woods, we stop at another bench for a breather. I'm hoping that the Budweiser fellow will pass us up, but he stops too, acting as if he is examining some nearby flora. While we rest, I read aloud to John from the brochure.

The nature of "Mystery Spot" is baffling and mystifying. Exercise caution when entering the vortex of "Mystery Spot." It is an anti-gravitational electromagnetic force field and could cause reactions.

I chuckle. "Remember that Wonder Spot in Wisconsin, dear? I think they said the same thing. The most dangerous part of it was the snack bar."

"Oh yeah," John says. "That was something."

I look up from the brochure. The path ahead is almost dark with foliage. At the end of it, I can see that there is a bright clearing. It's not that far really, but we still have a ways to go. As we continue walking, the Budweiser man stays fifty or sixty feet behind us. So John and I just walk along as briskly as we can. Rather, as briskly as I can. Along the path, there are signs:

ALMOST THERE!

"Hope I make it," I say to John. I keep up my pace. My hand is quivering a bit on my cane. Soon there is another sign:

YOU ARE ABOUT TO ENTER "MYSTERY SPOT"

We walk out into the clearing. It is wide and grassy and could be anywhere. "Looks like where we came in," I say, my breath coming fast and hard. But it's different. I realize this as we pause on the path. Not far ahead is a hill with a house, a little bungalow, settled on the side, as if it had slid down. The house could use a good coat of paint. The trees that surround it are like corkscrews twisted into the earth. I point them out to John as we walk. He just squints.

I look at the brochure. There is picture of a man and woman in "The House of Mystery." The walls of the house are straight, yet the couple's bodies are slanted at an impossible angle. Their feet are back behind their heads, reluctantly staying put, while their bodies are being pulled toward something else. I turn to show the picture to John, but he isn't there and I drop the brochure. When I go to pick it up, I start to feel very woozy. I clutch at my cane, put my weight on it, and it keeps me from toppling to the asphalt, but

I can no longer stand up. I feel myself dropping slowly to my knees. I brace myself for the excruciating pain that will come as they meet the ground. It never comes. My knees aren't the least bit sore. Even with everything that is happening, I am amazed that my legs actually feel good. In fact, my whole body feels better than it has in years, freer, as if a small part of me has lifted, the part that feels pain. The only problem is that my head is lighter too. I can't get up.

"John," I say, kneeling now, on my painless knees, both hands on the handle of my cane.

I turn around and see John ten or fifteen feet behind me, off the path. I can see that he feels something too, but not the same as me. He is in a daze, more so than usual.

"Ella?" he croaks, looking the wrong way, toward the Mystery House. "Where are you?"

I call out to him again. He is very lost. There are short periods like this at home. They used to be shorter. Now I watch my husband as he sits down on the lawn and starts to cry, every once in a while saying my name as if he is mourning me here on the edge of Nebraska at the amazing goddamned Mystery Spot.

"John!" I yell as loudly as I can. My head is clear now, knees almost completely supporting me, but I still can't get up. Finally, I feel the presence of another person next to me. I know who it is.

"Are you two tourists?" asks the Budweiser man. Not "Can I help?" or "Should I get an ambulance?"

"My husband doesn't feel well and I can't get up," I say, sharper than I usually speak to anyone.

"But are you guys tourists?" His voice is excited and skittery.

"Yes, we're tourists!" I scream. "Now would you please help me up?"

The idiot just stands there. He pulls a notebook from the pocket of his baggy shorts and starts to write in it. "I knew you were tourists because that's the only people this happens to. It doesn't bother us people who live around here."

I take a deep breath, swing my cane, and hit him right where it counts. He goes down like a sack of peat moss. While he is on the ground, writhing, I scooch over to him and yell into his right ear. "Will you please help us?" I have my cane poised over his head. I am pretty annoyed by this time. He frantically shakes his head yes. "Good," I say. "Now help me up."

The Budweiser man, holding his stomach, a little unsteady, slowly rises to his feet, then helps me to do the same. Surprisingly, once I am up, I don't need much assistance. I am still a bit dizzy, but my knees feel sturdy and strong, like a twenty-year-old's. We head over to John. I take one arm; the Budweiser man takes the other. John is able to walk all right. He's just very disoriented.

Back on the path, heading toward the shuttle stop, John keeps opening his eyes wide like he has seen something that startled him, but he is walking more on his own now. This is good, because the farther we get from the Mystery Spot, the harder it gets for me to hold him up, even a little. My knees are starting to feel how they usually feel. Worse. I look over at the Budweiser man. This man, whom I just smacked in the balls, has my husband on his arm and is walking very straight and proud, like we are all on the promenade at Atlantic City.

"You come to this place, even though you live around here?" I ask him.

"Sure. It's fun."

"You mean it's fun watching the tourists pass out."

He looks down at his shoes, like a child. "It doesn't happen to everyone. It's just that the nearer you get to the vortex, the less gravity there is. Plus the magnetic fields and all."

We get through the woods. John is walking now without any help. He seems fine, but my whole body hurts like hell. My knees are throbbing. John now starts to help me. The Budweiser man, finally untethered from the two of us, will not shut up.

"We're lighter here," he keeps saying. "There's not so much pulling us to the earth. But on the other hand, there's not so much holding us either. Some say it's a sort of deflection of gravitational force. But according to Newtonian theory—"

I interrupt. "Excuse us, but we've got to catch the shuttle. Thank you for the help."

"Uh-huh," says John. He seems like his old self. Well, maybe not his old self, but at least his recent self. And I will settle for that.

"Good*bye*," I say firmly to the Budweiser man.

It is just a little farther to the bench at the shuttle stop. Our friend reluctantly turns and starts back through the woods. I imagine he will continue his search for disoriented tourists in the area with the mysterious powers. We have already made his day. At the bench, we sit quietly. Then for no reason, John takes my hand and holds it in his.

We are the only ones on the shuttle, and we sit in the same seats as before. The same young man is driving. This time, he does not say anything over the PA. I wonder if he still feels great and ready. I know there are times when I feel ready, then I look at John and wonder how he will get along. I think about what the Budweiser man said: there is not so much holding us to the earth. Still, we hold on for as long as we can, for whatever our reasons. The driver drops us off by the ticket office.

As we head back to the van, John walks much faster than he usually does. I know he wants to get out of here, but I can't keep up, so I stop in the middle of the parking lot. Standing there, surrounded by all this gravel, I try not to feel what I am feeling. I look over at John. He is almost to the van when he notices that I am not with him. There is a flash of alarm in his eyes. Then I know that this is where we are heading, our own Mystery Spot, the eventual destination of all marriages, where one is without the other.

Finally, John looks over to where I am standing. After a few seconds, I start walking again. As I go around to my side of the van, I notice that someone has put a bumper sticker right above our license plate.

WE'VE BEEN TO
THE AMAZING "MYSTERY SPOT!"

Amazing, indeed.

Back on the freeway, there is no traffic. We drive like hell, try to put some miles between us and that place. And we do. Occasionally, I catch a glimpse of one of the gaudy signs in my rearview mirror, but I avert my eyes. Soon, there are no more signs. The miles roll past us, carry us, pull us with the irresistible force of distance.

We are at Disneyland by the next morning.

the listening room

*L*ucky. At that time, I'd heard the word used to describe a marble or a coin or a baseball mitt, but never a bed. Yet it was what I heard one Saturday night, eavesdropping on my parents' pinochle group. I had recently discovered that by sitting at the top of the stairs where the ceiling angled, I could hear what everyone in the living room was saying. Of course, with two card tables of adults, they were often talking or laughing at the same time, but within the scatter and volley of conversation, especially after a few rounds of highballs, there was plenty of information that was interesting to an eight-year-old boy.

In 1963, my parents had been married about ten years. They were six or seven years older than the other couples in their group and had already completed their family, which consisted of my two younger brothers and me. The other couples were all in their first few years of marriage and constantly looking to my parents for advice. The only other couple with children was the Phillipses, who had a one-year-old girl.

On this night, Mr. Phillips was ribbing the other two couples about taking too long to start their families.

"What are you two waiting for—Christmas?" he said, his voice booming. When he started laughing, he was the only one. That happened a lot.

"We just now decided that this was the right time," said Mr. Stahl, a soft-spoken man who had recently started smoking a pipe, but even I could tell that he hadn't quite grown into it yet.

"Uh-huh," said Mrs. Stahl, whose squeaky voice reminded me of Felix the Cat.

"Well, don't wait too long," said Mr. Phillips, laughing again. "Pretty soon, you'll be too old."

"Oh, shut up, Jim," said Mrs. Phillips. She often said this and everyone always laughed. They did it this time as well.

My father could not pass up this opportunity to dispense some wisdom. I recognized the tone of his voice. "You know, sometimes these things take time."

"Did it take you two long, Stan?" asked Mr. Stahl.

"A while."

"But then, we've got the lucky bed," I heard my mother say.

I could hear the shock in my father's voice. "*Jess,* for God's sake."

"What?" My mother was always bewildered when my father would scold her for saying something "bohemian."

"You don't have to tell everyone, you know," said my father, under his breath.

"Too late for that," said Mr. Phillips, hooting. "Come on, fill us in."

My mother must have rolled her eyes. "Oh relax, Stan. We're all adults here. Everyone's married, what's the difference?"

"Just never mind," hissed my father.

"You might as well tell us," said Mr. Phillips.

"Yeah, come on," said Mr. Thibideau. "Tell us. This sounds sexy."

By this time, I was about falling over the banister, trying to hear everything, though I had no idea what they were talking about. All I knew was that I wasn't supposed to be hearing it.

"Oh, there's nothing really to tell," said my father, quickly now, trying to get the whole thing over and done with. "It's just that all the kids were, well, conceived, in the bed in the spare room."

"Not your regular . . . place?" Mrs. Stahl managed to squeak out.

"Nope. That's how we know it's lucky," proclaimed my mother, proudly.

"That is odd," said Mr. Stahl. "Three kids, none of them, uh, *in your own bed.*"

I was confused by all the hemming and hawing going on down there. Then the whispering began, followed by long bursts of raucous, surprised laughter, like when they listened to the Rusty Warren *Knockers Up!* records.

The verb *conceive* was foreign to me at that time, but I did know about my mother and father sleeping in the spare room. Although I knew they loved each other, my parents constantly bickered. All it took was for my mother to do something in a way my father considered incorrect. It could be anything, really, like washing the dishes in lukewarm, instead of scalding hot water. He would say something like, "For Christ's sakes, Jess, what were you thinking?"

"Go to hell," my mother would reply.

He would stomp out of the room, then stomp right back in. "You know, I'm just trying to help," he'd say.

"If you really want to help, mind your own goddamned business," she would say. Then they'd yell at each other until my father stormed out again. Five minutes later, he'd be back to apologize, to ask my mother *can we be friends again?* She'd laugh and everything would be fine. This was pretty much their routine. But if they fought before bed, my mother would scuffle over to the spare room in a huff. The wife leaving the bedroom was the opposite of what I saw on television, but that was how it worked in our house.

The part I didn't know about was my father going to the spare room to apologize.

With all the laughter and hushed conversation going on downstairs, I couldn't hear anything that was said. Then suddenly, the noise died down and I heard the quavering voice of a woman. It was Babs Thibideau, the quietest member of the group.

"We've been trying for a year now with no luck," she said, her voice breaking. "I don't know what we're doing wrong."

Even from upstairs, I felt the mood change. There was a gush of support, everyone telling Mrs. Thibideau that it was all right, that sometimes these things happened. Miracle doctors' names were mentioned, secret how-to books suggested. Even Jim Phillips, who was always first to give anyone the business, said they shouldn't feel bad. Still, none of this prepared anyone for what happened next.

"Why don't you two try the lucky bed?" said my mother.

It got very quiet. I was upstairs, confused, but even I knew something important had happened. I heard more whispering, then Mr. Phillips saying, "Well, you can't argue with success."

"Then it's settled," said my mother. "You'll come over and stay in the spare room. I'll fix it up special for you. It would be our pleasure."

My father said nothing.

That night, I could barely sleep, unsure of what any of it meant. Of course, I had seen my mother pregnant and had asked questions. After a few unsatisfying answers, I had let it rest, not really caring that much. Now I wanted to know. *Why would anyone need a lucky bed?*

My parents mentioned nothing at the breakfast table Sunday morning. I couldn't ask anything without revealing myself. There was nothing to do but fret about it, my strategy for most everything. As a child, worry was my best friend. It never left me. It would settle in my chest and stay there all day, a vague ache. At night, I cuddled up with my worry like a favorite stuffed animal. And here—*here* was plenty to worry about. I wished that I had never heard anything about the bed in our spare room.

With three children, it was amazing that we even had a spare room, but there was no shortage of space in our house, a rambling, echoing colonial across the street from a Catholic school. Our house had once been home to a covey of chaste women, a flock of nuns—the notoriously sadistic Sisters of Saint Rita. Although we weren't Catholic, the history of the house often made itself evident in subtle, eerie ways—a dot of ancient candle wax on a window sill, a lost rosary bead wedged under a toe molding, the station of the cross mounted on the wall by the stairway. I had always felt an otherworldly presence in our house. Now I sensed something else.

The spare room was where boxes and stray furniture collected, where I used to hide from my little brothers. That afternoon, I decided to look around in there. All I knew about the lucky bed was that it had been left here by the nuns. All us kids had nun beds, hard as hell, and I couldn't see what made this one so different from my own. I looked around and noticed a few rumpled tissues on the floor. I examined them, fretted about them, then decided they were from when my mother was sleeping there with a cold. I did notice that, unlike my parents' room, the spare room had a working lock on the door.

After a week or so, I began to forget about the lucky bed. My worry had diminished to a warm white marble that nestled comfortably between my lungs. I was settling back into ignorance, a welcome relief. Then, on a Monday night, after my brothers had reluctantly been put to bed and I knew it would soon be time for me, the doorbell rang. My mother answered the door and did not seem at all surprised to see the Thibideaus. Yet, there was no high-pitched *Hi!* the way she always greeted people when they visited our house for dinner or pinochle. Mr. Thibideau was carrying a small valise. The marble between my lungs expanded to the size of a softball.

"Babs. Milt," my father said gravely, as he approached them. He didn't shake Mr. Thibideau's hand or embrace Mrs. Thibideau. He just took their jackets and hung them in our front closet.

The Thibideaus smiled as they stood there, but I could see they were uncomfortable.

"Do you want some coffee?" offered my mother.

"That would be nice," said Mrs. Thibideau.

My father looked at all three of them. "Maybe a highball?"

"*Yes please,*" said Mr. Thibideau. His wife nodded emphatically.

At that point, my mother sent me up to bed. I pretended not to hear her and followed my father into the kitchen.

While my father made the drinks, I asked him, "Dad, are Mr. and Mrs. Thibideau staying over?"

"Uh-huh," he said, pouring shots of Canadian Club into four tumblers stacked with ice.

"What for?"

"We're just having a little pajama party, kiddo," he said, topping off the glasses with Vernors ginger ale. The kitchen smelled spicy-sweet and pungent. "They'll be gone tomorrow. Shouldn't you be in bed?"

"You've never done this before."

He looked at me and sighed. "Sure we have."

"When?"

"Before you were born."

"But—"

"Time for bed."

While the adults drank their highballs, I perched at the top of the stairs—

scared and excited—and listened in. It was the most boring conversation I had ever eavesdropped: *the weather, lawns, are you going to get your address painted on the curb?*

Finally, Mr. Thibideau yawned loudly and said it was time to hit the hay. I looked at the clock in the hallway. It was nine fifteen. My bedtime was nine o'clock, but our household didn't usually shut down until after the eleven o'clock news and the first fifteen minutes of Johnny Carson. I slithered downstairs on the pretense of getting a glass of water.

My mother intercepted me on my way to the refrigerator. "I thought I told you to go to bed," she said.

"Aren't you going to tuck me in?" I asked, though I had recently complained that I was getting too old for it.

"All right. Let me get our guests settled. And then you're next, mister."

So after my mother got the Thibideaus arranged up in the spare room, she came back downstairs and told me to get washed up and ready for bed. I went into the den to say good night to my father and managed to waste more time watching television. It was nine forty-five when my mother found me. She ordered me to brush my teeth and put on my pajamas.

As soon as I walked upstairs, I could hear faint sounds coming from the spare bedroom: squeak of bedsprings, a voice out of breath, panting, a grunt. Something was wrong, I thought, someone was hurt. I almost rushed downstairs to tell my mother, then somehow knew this would be wrong, the act of a child. Confused, I walked faster to get past the room. When the floor creaked beneath me, I heard someone say in a strained voice, *not so loud.*

In the bathroom, I turned on the water full blast as I brushed my teeth. I raced into my room, twisted off my clothes, tugged on my pajamas, tried to ignore the hushed rhythmic terror of what was going on behind the wall, ten feet away. Inside my room with the door closed, I was afraid to leave and afraid to stay, but I knew I had to say good night to my parents. I ran out, closed the door loudly behind me and fled downstairs.

"Good night, big boy," said my father, looking up from the television.

"Still want me to tuck you in?" asked my mother, closing her book momentarily, finger still holding her place on the page.

I was about to shake my head no, because I was afraid to let anyone hear what was going on upstairs. I felt it was somehow my fault. Yet my biggest fear was not that I would get in trouble, it was that she would explain it all to me. That would have been too horrible. Still, a part of me, despite my fears, wanted answers.

As my mother and I walked upstairs, we could hear the noises, quieter now, but still very much there. I kept waiting for her to say something about *all this racket,* the way she would with us kids, but she didn't say a word. In the hallway, she stared straight ahead, beaming in a way I'd never seen before. It certainly was not the smile I received when I showed her a good report card or crayon portrait, but something else altogether—a smile of quiet delight that told me my mother was not going to explain a thing to me. She squeezed my hand and opened the door to my room.

"Come on, sweetie. Time for bed."

I jumped in and she pulled the covers up under my chin and kissed me goodnight. There was still noise as she closed the door to my room. I heard her footfalls on the hallway runner like I did every night; then they stopped. After a long minute, her steps resumed as she headed back downstairs.

Suddenly things went silent and I could hear only whispering from the spare room. I could also hear my brother Lint, in the room far down the hall, blissfully oblivious to it all, five years old and snoring away, victim of adenoids and perpetual sniffles. I don't know what would have happened had he heard anything, perhaps a tantrum, or complete indifference. I stuffed my head under the covers until I couldn't breathe. When I came up for air, everything was quiet and I went to sleep.

The Thibideaus were gone by the time I got up for school. Everyone acted like everything was normal. In school that day, my homeroom teacher yelled at me for not paying attention to social studies, for being what she called "moony-eyed." I was afraid of what was going to happen when I got home from school. But when I got there, nothing happened. My mother was making dinner and my brothers were running around, making noise as usual. My father came home and we ate dinner. After a few days of familial grind, the ache again subsided and the lucky bed became something that maybe never happened.

Another Monday night: three weeks later, two days after my parents' pinochle group met at the Phillipses'. I was lying in bed, unable to sleep, fretting about someone at school who had threatened to beat me up, when I heard a knock downstairs. The front door opened and I heard murmured greetings from the vestibule. Dread welled in my stomach. *It couldn't be.*

Minutes later, I heard them all trundle up the stairs. I started to have difficulty breathing. Even whispering, I could recognize the cartoon voice of Mrs. Stahl. My mother showed them to the spare room and shut the door without even saying goodnight. Then I heard her walk toward my room, so I closed my eyes till I could just see images through my eyelashes. As my mother reached to close my door, I saw her face just for a moment in the golden dim of the hallway. She was smiling.

Before long, the noise started. A bump, then a high pitched *ow,* then laughter, and the clack of bedsprings slowly at first, then faster, then stopping. I heard more laughter, muffled now, the springs again, then air being inhaled quickly and repeatedly, which sounded to me like fright returning again and again—then the springs creaking so fast that they no longer made noise—invisible obbligato to the bump of the bed against the wall and the ebb and swell of my gastric fluids. Then in the middle of it all, I heard my youngest brother, Steverino, who was only three, wander out into the hall. He yelled for my mother from the top of the stairs, and all the noise stopped. I heard her come up and put him back in bed, tell him everything was all right. After all that, I felt very sick. I couldn't understand why my parents let this go on. I realized, head beneath blanket, that I could no longer trust them.

When I went down to breakfast the next morning, I was very tired. During the night, the ache had spread to my bones, pulling me again and again from my ragged sleep. The idea of going to school, with its attendant worries, bullies, crazy teachers, etc., actually appealed to me. Then, there at the kitchen table, with my father and my brothers and their usual cereal mess and squall, were the Stahls. I couldn't believe it.

"Hey, kiddo, how'd you sleep last night?" asked my father, buttering some toast for me, his newspaper folded into a neat rectangle on the table, like everything was just fine and dandy.

"Okay."

The Stahls said good morning, acted as if nothing at all had happened. I didn't ask how they came to be sitting at my kitchen table at seven a.m., but there they were, gobbling down eggs and bacon, as if they hadn't already devoured each other last night.

My mother was at the stove, very nearly glowing.

The Thursday after, the Phillipses were over. They came for dinner without their baby girl and I knew it was going to happen again. It wasn't bad though. Mrs. Phillips helped me do the dishes and Mr. Phillips kidded around with me, which I didn't really like. He kept saying *hey punk,* and pushing me around. I got that enough at school. They watched television with us. Then my mother put my brothers to bed and told me to start getting ready myself.

That night, I almost couldn't stay awake long enough. The Phillipses didn't go to bed until well after midnight and they made much less noise than the others did. The bed played its squeak song, but quieter. There was whispering, lots of whispering, nothing I could understand, the same way my mother and father spoke to each other when they embraced in front of us kids. Once I asked my mother what she had whispered to my father. "None of your business," she had said.

The Phillipses did not take long. I wrapped my pillow around my head.

A few days later, the Thibideaus were back "just to make sure," I heard someone say. Then the Phillipses again, out of turn, I recall thinking at the time. No one stayed for breakfast again. I think my parents got tired of making excuses to my brothers. No further explanations were offered to me. Nor did I request them. But a curious thing happened in the middle of all this: our household, with all its chaos and clamor, was in some inexplicable way, being calmed. My brothers, whom I should mention were mostly asleep when our visitors arrived, were perhaps most affected. Of course, they still acted like three- and five-year-old boys—tantrums, boo-boos, squabbles— but mostly they behaved, as if gripped by something that kept them in a gurgly state of lassitude.

Perhaps this all could be explained by the change in my parents. My mother was absolutely radiant during this period, congenial to everything and everyone. She whistled as she cooked dinner, fussed over my father, hugged us kids until we had to run away. It was the only time she was even remotely like the mothers we saw on TV. She stopped cursing at my father. My dad, too, was acting differently. He came home from work on time each day, never any drinks with the boys. Saturday golf took a back seat to family outings. He helped around the house, helped with our homework. Bickering was at an all time low.

The only person who hadn't truly settled in was me. The strained cries and half-grunts that trembled our nite-lited hall may have became commonplace, but they still disturbed me. Eventually I realized that the lucky bed posed no threat to me, but somehow I still felt in harm's way. The lump of worry in my chest dissolved into my bloodstream, an aggressive virus now, an infection shoving its way through my body, its bacteria collecting on the tender leaves of my eight-year-old heart. It didn't seem fair, especially while everyone else in the house was so disgustingly cheerful. I noticed my parents were spending time in the spare room themselves—pilfered moments when they would put me in charge of watching my brothers, slipping me quarters to keep me conscientious. They were very quiet about it, but I knew what they were doing up there. Although I didn't really, and I certainly didn't have a name for it, but still I *knew.* Something was happening in my house and I felt its presence.

What I know now was that sex was seeping into the woodwork of our old nunnery like the scent of a foreign delicacy, some perplexingly funky curry wafting through our hallways from under the door of the spare room. With this many people doing it under our roof, sex could no longer be obscured by the odors of dusty domesticity, spit-up, and lilac Glade air freshener. When guests were over, sometimes I could smell what was going on through the heating registers. Even without a true understanding, even through my fear, it was starting to fascinate me. I knew the most intimate secrets of my parents' friends, though I did not intuit the act, only the intimacy. I knew who the screamers were, the whimperers, the dirty talkers. I knew who spoke to God over and over. (I knew it couldn't have been the same God to whom I spoke as I laid me down to sleep.)

Through all this, we just carried on, went about our normal business. There we were: a snapshot of the perfect American family—my mother vacuuming, grinning like a dipsomaniac; my father going to work at Ford's, reading the paper; me doing my homework; my brothers watching TV, socking each other. While upstairs, Babs and Milt Thibideau rut furiously behind the door of our spare bedroom.

No, there was nothing at all strange going on.

One Saturday afternoon, I walked upstairs and saw that the door to the spare room was open. When I walked in, I noticed my father's feet extended from under the lucky bed, as if he were a mechanic beneath our '61 Fairlane.

"Dad?"

My father had been doing something under the bed, I could tell from the way his feet had been shifting. But now, hearing my voice, his body was still.

"Vance?" he said.

I leaned down and looked under the bed. "What are you doing, Dad?" I noticed the oilcan.

"It's just these bed springs—" He stopped himself. "Hey, would you do me a favor? How about going down to the basement to get me a medium screwdriver?"

"Okay."

"Thanks, kiddo."

When I came back upstairs, he was in a different room, their bedroom, standing by the doorway. He took the screwdriver from me and removed the chrome plate from the light switch. He looked inside.

"We've been having a problem with this switch," he said, boosting me up to where the switch plate was.

We both knew he knew nothing about wiring and that there was really no problem, but we played at it, peering deep into the dim recesses of our walls, both content to be away from the other room and what it meant. Still, I half-expected to hear furtive sounds escape from the hole in the wall.

"Seems to be all right now," my father said.

"Yup," I said.

I was sleeping when the doorbell rang at ten forty-five one Thursday night. I woke up right away, having become attuned to nocturnal sounds. As my father opened the front door, I sneaked to the top of the stairs. Had he not spoken their names, I would have never known it was Doug and Judy Keohane, who were not officially part of my parents' pinochle group, but substitutes for the Stahls, who had to drop out for two months the year before, while Bud Stahl (*OhOhOhOhOoohhhh!*) recovered from a double hernia operation. My mother sounded surprised to see them. I don't think she was expecting company.

I could hear Judy Keohane's stage whisper from upstairs. Her voice was slightly slurred, the way I knew adults sounded after a few highballs.

"Jess. Please help us. We heard that Babs Thibideau is pregnant. We know about the bed."

My mother stammered. "Well, I'm not really—"

"Please. We're desperate, Jess."

At this point, I knew my parents were exchanging those *should we? shouldn't we?* looks that they exchanged when I wanted something very badly. Yet I had a feeling my mother would give in. When she did, I padded back to my room, as quickly as possible.

On their way up, I heard Mr. Keohane stumble on a step, then laugh. After my mother got them settled in, I lay in bed, telling myself I should go back to sleep, but knowing that I would wait for the show. But there was no show, no panting or laughter or groaning. The bed never touched the wall. There was quiet for a long time, then loud whispering, and I heard Mrs. Keohane distinctly say, "You'll have to do better than that."

"Shut your goddamn mouth," hissed Mr. Keohane.

"Listen to the big man," she said, laughing aloud now.

There was no more whispering. "I thought I told you to shut up!" shouted Mr. Keohane.

Down the hall, I heard Steverino whimpering in his bed.

"You fucking whore," said Mr. Keohane.

I heard these things: a blow—a closed hand against a face; a short yelp; a single creak of the bed; sobbing. I heard the door of my parents' room click open and I heard my father's knock on the door of the spare room.

Mr. Keohane got up to open the door. My father asked if everything was all right. Mr. Keohane said everything was fine, just fine. There was a long silence, punctuated only by Mrs. Keohane's snuffling. Then I heard my father tell them that it was time for them to leave.

"Well, Stan, we haven't really done what we came for," stammered Mr. Keohane.

"I think you've done more than enough," I heard my father say.

I listened to my father lead the two of them downstairs and out our front door. I don't think he even let them put their street clothes on. The Keohanes never came back to our house. Nor did anyone use the lucky bed after that, except for my parents, who were to have one more child, my accidental youngest brother Rudy, who drowned in a kiddy pool in our backyard when he was four. I never knew if he was conceived in the lucky bed.

Two of the women in my parents' pinochle group were pregnant that fall. Not that I fully understood the connection between the occurrences of that spring and someone having a child. Everything: the noises I heard, the terror I felt, my mother's behavior, all seemed secret and separate, events that couldn't possibly connect in nature. It was a long time before I understood. Even in my teens, when I studied the process with a smoldering intensity, elements were always missing from the equation. When I finally did grasp it all, the fear returned to riddle me like a cancer, all through my college years. The actual experience: is it any surprise that I was much older than most when it happened?

For years, I was only truly comfortable listening or watching—the most important thing I learned away at college. You could easily conclude that I was, perhaps still am, backward, or at the very least, twisted sideways. Even after I reached my late thirties, after I met Diane, the woman who consented to marry me, peccadilloes and all, who even indulges my predilections on occasion with strangers we meet online, even then I said nothing to my parents about the lucky bed. Although middle age is the time when the child should ask the parents the questions he's always meant to ask, while there's still time.

Then my father died and my mother decided to sell the old house. It was sad, but the place had long been too big for two people and was now, with its teetering staircases, ragged runners, and unforgiving hardwood floors, uninhabitable for one elderly woman. The place sold immediately and she needed a place to stay for a few months before she could move into her new Assisted Living apartment in Garden City. My brothers' families are sizable and neither had the extra living space. With no children, Diane and I were the logical choice.

Picking her up at the old house, she asked me to take her upstairs to look around one last time. What could I do? Because of her condition, she hadn't been properly able to say her goodbyes to the place.

During the endless, torturous climb up the stairs, holding on to my mother as she clutched the varnish-worn banister with a death grip, I felt myself gripped by something I had hoped to avoid.

Once upstairs, we walked slowly through the hallway, our steps tiny and shuffling. It was there, with my mother grasping my forearm for support, that I experienced a frisson—a magnesium flash igniting a chain of recollections as charged as a string of firecrackers. I don't know exactly what caused it— the particular reflection of light on the hallway walls, the labored rasp of the floor, the air thick with heated dust, or maybe it was the actual physical arousal I felt. Perhaps my father's death was a catalyst, the process of two persons becoming one moving me to something, I don't know.

I turned to my mother to ask her about the lucky bed, to tell her everything I knew about it, how it had scared me, how it had changed me. But when I faced her, I couldn't say a word.

"Are you all right?" my mother asked.

I quickly nodded yes, assuming it would pass for grief. We walked a few steps farther, past the spare room. That was where my mother looked at me and smiled, the smile I had not seen since my childhood, the one I was never supposed to see.

noise of the heart

there was a thundering in Leland's ears as he attempted, with unsteady hands, to work his way behind the bookcase to where the telephone was connected. There was a small box on the floor in front of him. He kept glancing at the disclaimer on the back of the box. It was giving him the creeps:

This Telephone Surveillance device is not intended for the unauthorized interception or recording of wire communications and should not be used for those purposes. This device is to be used only in a legal and lawful manner in accordance with all applicable FCC regulations.

"Fuck the FCC," said Leland aloud. The sound of his own voice startled him for a moment, as he disconnected the phone cord from the wall jack. Somehow the FCC wasn't a concern when your wife was working late three nights a week. Or taking off for six hours on a Saturday and coming back with an excuse about getting her hair styled. Or maybe the FCC could investigate the piece of foil he found in her purse that he was pretty sure was from a condom.

Leland fitted the cord from the back of their phone into the Spy Shop Model 2800 Auto-Telephone Recorder, then after fumbling a few times behind the bookcase, connected the recorder cord into the modular wall jack. He plugged the recorder into the electrical outlet, turned it on, and slid it behind the bookcase, out of sight, but where he could access it when necessary. Now the phone would record all incoming and outgoing calls. He would find out exactly what was going on. The FCC could prosecute him after that.

It was a long shot anyway. Whatever was going on was being conducted strictly on Madeline's cell phone. It was ringing an awful lot at home these days and she wasn't taking the calls in front of Leland. It had gotten to the point that he felt physically ill every time he heard her ring tone, a digitized version of "Call Me" by Al Green. Of course, he could just ask Madeline what was going on, but that was too terrifying. Besides, he already had an idea of what the answer was. All this was really just to get him to believe what was probably already true.

Two days later, there were five calls on the tape, but he didn't want to listen to it at home. The only other place he could play it was in his car, a six-year-old Beetle that had a cassette deck along with the CD player and radio. A lucky break, because who the hell had a cassette player these days?

He listened to the first two calls as he drove through Royal Oak, looking at all the over-caffeinated people sipping lattes in outdoor cafes. Both calls were from Madeline's mother, first reminding her that they were supposed to go shopping, then calling back to confirm the time. Talking to her mother, Madeline sounded distant and distracted, even annoyed. She sounded the same way on the third call talking to Leland, when he called from work to tell her that he was going to be a little late. One call was from the Institute of Arts, asking for donations, and yet another from Madeline's mother. That was it.

Two days later, he listened to the most recent calls as he drove aimlessly down 8 Mile, past the U Buy We Fry fish joints, the topless bars, and the storefront churches. Six calls, all from Madeline's mom, Leland, and people who wanted money. Apparently they were the only ones who used their landline these days. This wasn't working, thought Leland.

That night about four a.m., Leland quietly extricated himself from the twisted, dampish sheets on his side and got up from bed.

Madeline stirred. "Where are you going, Lee?" she asked drowsily.

"I can't sleep. I'm going to watch some TV."

"Close the door."

On a small table by the vestibule was Madeline's cell phone on its charger cord. He picked it up, flipped it open, hit the call button and scrolled the history. Besides all the expected numbers, there were several numbers he didn't recognize. He thought about writing them all down, but instead he took the phone in both hands and twisted it until he heard something crack.

Madeline went to work the next day without even noticing. That night, she mentioned that her cell had died. At work, they were in the process of getting her a new one.

His plan worked. Two days later, while driving on the Southfield freeway, Leland heard it—a call from a strange man who spoke with great familiarity to his wife. His pulse quickened as he listened. *How are you? Where are you now? I want to see you, are you free later . . .*

That was really all Leland could listen to before he hit the eject button. The radio snapped on loud, playing a horrible Kool & the Gang song. Leland felt ill. He pushed the tape back in, then turned it off just before it started playing again. He didn't want to listen to any more of it, but he had to. There wasn't much more. *When can you meet? Friday night.* Madeline's voice sounded relaxed and casual. *Will you be able to manage it? Yes, don't worry.*

That was it. It was all very businesslike. There was no *I need you, I want you to fuck me, fuck me now, I'm yearning for you* . . . None of that.

His name was Jim.

Leland turned off the cassette deck and pulled over to the side of the freeway. There were men from the Wayne County Road Commission in orange vests cleaning up trash along the grassy slope of the freeway. One of them stopped to look at him. Leland was breathing heavily and sweating by that time, his head pounding. The cars driving past sounded like jet planes taking off. What the hell was happening? He hadn't planned his life this way. Driving around while listening to the personal phone conversations of his wife. Strike that, listening to personal phone conversations of his wife and her lover.

Lover. What a silly word. He and Madeline used to make fun of that word. When they first met, she had a friend, Trish the Dish, who would always introduce some guy as *her lover.* She was trying to be exotic, but it just sounded ridiculous. He and Madeline had always cracked up over it. They had even made up a name of an imaginary international lover of Trish's: Remy Fontaine. *This is my lover, Remy Fontaine,* Madeline would say in a fake Eurotrash accent. Then they would laugh until they were out of breath.

Yet the word applied here, with all its exotic connotations. My wife has a lover, Leland said aloud, as if he could not believe it until he heard it. The sound of the word ached his ears. *Lah*-ver, he said, touching his tongue to the roof of his mouth, then pursing his lips, kissing the air. The air did not kiss back.

Leland didn't listen to any more tapes for a few days. He didn't have the heart for it. When he got home from work Thursday, Madeline was at the kitchen sink, her back to him, putting away plates from the dishwasher. She stood there, stacking bowls on shelves, sorting flatware into the drawer, telling him about her day—some stupid thing a client had said, a new account they had just landed. Just then, Leland noticed how attractive she was looking these days. Today, her mahogany hair was turned upward in a flip and she was wearing a dress of a shiny fabric that subtly displayed her figure.

Madeline turned and faced him halfway when she gave him the lie.

"I'm going to get together with some people from work tomorrow night," she said, inserting knives into the rack. "We're just going to have a few drinks and bitch about work. So I won't be home until later." She turned all the way around and smiled at him.

Leland openly examined her face. He had never really heard a lie before, knowing it was a lie at the time. She didn't notice him staring at her. "Where are you going to go?" he asked.

"We don't know yet. Probably Royal Oak. We'll figure it out later." She turned to grab another dish.

He wanted to tell her that he knew, but could not make a sound. It was so strange, watching her lie to him. She was very good at it.

Friday night, Madeline was gone and Leland decided to listen to the latest tape at home. He sat at the dining room table with an old Sony Walkman of Madeline's that he had found in a box in the basement. Scanning through, he had found only one conversation with Madeline and *him*. She must have called while Leland was still at work. Another short conversation: *I'm looking forward to seeing you Friday night. Me too. Any problem? No, he believes me when I tell him.*

Leland ran to the bathroom to throw up. He did not quite make it and spent a good part of the next hour scrubbing the carpet with Lysol. He didn't listen to the rest of the tape. He put it away with the other one. After that, Leland went up to their bedroom, lay down, and did not wake up until he heard the front door open. He pretended that he was asleep.

"Lee, are you awake?" she asked, shedding clothes as she lay down next to him. He said nothing, just kept his eyes closed. He wanted to turn over to see her, to see what his wife looked like after she was with her *lover,* but could not bring himself to move, afraid of what he might see or smell. Instead, he just groaned and drew his own sour-smelling arm closer to his face and kept pretending to be asleep. She drew up closer him and he could smell liquor on her breath. What clothes she still had on smelled of cigarette smoke. She reached over and unbuckled his pants. Leland suddenly forgot to be asleep.

Leland loathed himself the next day. Just the slightest bit of coaxing and he gives in to her. But he wasn't entirely ashamed since it was the first time they had had sex in months and it was incredible. What had happened at her tryst? It tortured him to even think about it, that she had been with him, then Leland. And let's not even get into the disease part. What was going on? Had Madeline become insatiable? She certainly hadn't been that way before. They had both been perfectly satiable. Often, she didn't even seem that interested in sex. On the rare occasion when Leland felt courageous, he would try to initiate, and she would promptly nip it in the bud. When it did happen, it was always at her urging, like last night.

Whatever had happened, there was no chance to talk about it. She was gone in the morning. The note on the kitchen table:

Lee—
Have to work today. Home for dinner.
—Mad

Leland was alone for the day, with nothing to do but listen to the most recent tape, to whatever might have happened in the past day. After breakfast, a shower, getting dressed, after doing anything he could possibly think of, he sat down with the Walkman. But first, he listened to an old Sonny Boy Williamson tape that he found in the same box as the tape player. He enjoyed it until he got to the song "Checkin' Up on My Baby."

Great. Irony. Just what he needed right now. He ejected the tape, but still didn't listen to the new one. Instead, he went to Target to do a little shopping.

When he got back at about two in the afternoon, Madeline was home from work. Only he was pretty sure that she was never really at work. He had nothing to base that hunch on, just instinct. She was acting like everything was fine. Because everything *is* fine for her, thought Leland. She's got her husband, her faithful roommate, the man who doesn't say anything no matter what she does. And she has *him*—her lover, her *inamorato*, her back door man . . .

"Had to work today, huh," said Leland blankly, as he grabbed a glass from the cupboard, then filled it at the sink. He could hear the old pendulum clock in the next room clack away the moments and it gave the whole scene a theatricality that he didn't at all care for.

Madeline grimaced as she watched him. "God, Lee. I told you. Don't drink that tap water. It's full of lead and carcinogens. Jesus." She fetched a pitcher of filtered water from the refrigerator and poured him a fresh glass. "Here. Drink this. It's cold and clean."

"Thanks." He took the glass from her. The water was so cold, it practically hurt his hand to hold it. Behind him, the fridge quivered, then thumped alive. The sound irritated him.

Madeline looked at him, through him. "We are so busy now. I can't believe how much work I have. We've got another new business pitch next week."

Leland wanted to give her a deeply meaningful look, but as he was doing so, he inhaled some saliva and started coughing.

"Did you try to call?" said Madeline.

"Yes," he lied.

"Did you leave a message?"

"No." Leland was suddenly sure that she didn't go to work. It's amazing, he thought, all you need is to know once when someone is lying to you. From that point on, you will always know. Still, he'd confirm later when he checked the tape. Leland took a long drink of the icy water. His temples throbbed.

There was no rendezvous Friday night, Leland discovered later. At the last minute, it had been changed to Saturday morning. She must have actually gone out with people from work, after being ready to meet him all day. Hence the late night grope with Leland, who was merely convenient.

Harder and harder to listen to the tapes: never anything explicit or even near it—no mentions of the night before; no pet names; no aural close-ups of dewy hands intertwined; no whispers of positions successfully replicated from the *Kama Sutra;* no descriptions of stratovolcanic orgasms. What gave? For some reason, Leland wanted, needed something like that. Then maybe he could truly grasp the whole thing. From Jim, the outside man, he heard only murmured concerns: *What did you tell him? Will it be all right?*

Leland had more expected a mocking disrespect of the cuckold, how the sap didn't suspect a thing. Instead, Jim seemed more concerned about Leland's feelings than Madeline did, as if he sensed the gravity of the situation more so than she. He was always asking what she told Leland. Madeline would tell him, but you could detect the edge of irritation in her voice.

Leland realized this: to Madeline, he was hardly worth mentioning, an inconvenience, a nonentity. He had heard about people who unconsciously coordinate the demise of their relationship—the love note left in the pocket, the assignation where someone is sure to see. This wasn't one of those. It was more that Madeline just didn't give a shit. She lied, sure, to avoid the inevitable scene, to keep things from happening until they were right for her.

In the meantime, Leland wasn't anything to fret about. She knew he trusted her and would believe everything she said.

Except, thought Leland, here I am recording her phone conversations. Apparently, she is wrong about me.

Monday's tape:

Are you able to get away on Thursday? I think I can. Your house? Around six? I want to see you. Me too. Don't forget the thing. I won't.

"The thing? What the hell is the thing?" screamed Leland, there in the car, on the freeway. *The thing?* Sweet screaming Jesus, he could have lived with everything up to now if it hadn't been for that. What could *the thing* possibly be? *Birth control device? Double-pronged dildo? Cheese tray?* So many possibilities flashed through Leland's head, he couldn't keep track.

"I need details," Leland said, to no one in particular. He needed to know how long this affair was going to take. Would it just end and Madeline would be his wife again? Could he even deal with that? Leland now noticed that he was going eighty-seven miles per hour on the Southfield freeway, where the speed limit is sixty-five. Something had to be done.

Leland decided to go to the doctor. He really hadn't been feeling all that well lately, lots of headaches and trouble sleeping. In the back of his mind, he also hoped that his doctor might somehow help his situation. Leland knew he was thinking of an old-fashioned doctor, the kind who is happy to help with any problem—heal the soul, mend the spirit, that sort of thing. Did the horrible ache you felt because your wife had another *mule kickin' in her stall* come under that category? Leland wondered how he might bring up the subject.

After the weigh-in and the urine sample, a dry-lipped nurse led Leland to the examination room, instructed him to remove his shirt, socks, and shoes, and lie on the examining table. After drawing blood, the nurse stuck adhesive pads to various parts of Leland's body and hooked him up to the echocardiogram machine. After gathering the results, she disengaged Leland and reminded him to remove his pants.

As she wheeled the machine from the room, she said, "Doctor Tom will be in shortly." (This was what the doctor's patients called him, for his name was so painfully long and Polish, so laden with the more obscure consonants, no one could bear the burden required for the constant correct pronunciation of it, including the good doc himself.) After ten minutes of sitting in his underwear, the doctor burst into the examination room, brimming with ruddy bonhomie.

"How are you feeling these days, Leland?" asked the doctor.

"Oh, just great, Doctor Tom," lied Leland, just as heartily. (He hated not being as robust as the person to whom he was speaking.)

"Great, great. Glad to hear it."

Doctor Tom checked Leland's ears, throat, eyes, and nose, then his reflexes (a bit sluggish, but all right). While Leland was trying to figure out some way to broach the subject of his wife's infidelities, Doctor Tom listened to Leland's lungs, his arteries, and then his heart.

"How's it sound, Doc?" asked Leland.

Doctor Tom smiled. "Give a listen."

Smiling back, Leland took the stethoscope, inserted the tips in his own ears. He was not prepared for what he heard—a loathsome, horrible, *splenching* sound that nearly caused him to upchuck right there in the examination room.

"That's your heart," said Doctor Tom, making a notation, not noticing the utter collapse of his patient's face. He took the stethoscope back and proceeded to take Leland's blood pressure. At that point, Leland was barely conscious of the pressure on his arm, then its release.

The doctor looked up at him, not trying to hide his alarm. "Your blood pressure is way up."

Leland glanced at the doctor, distracted. "I guess I'm just a little nervous about the physical. I've been under a lot of stress lately."

"Hmm," he said, with a kind of gravitas that was meant to let Leland know that he was not at all pleased.

Leland did not notice the doctor's tone. All he could think about was his heart and the repulsive flatulent sound it had emitted.

A few minutes later, after the doctor had examined Leland's body for suspicious moles and made him turn his head and cough, he took his blood pressure again. It was slightly better, still not good, but at least Leland wasn't ready for the emergency room. He took it once more at the end of the physical, just as Leland was about to get dressed. Only then was it closer to normal, which seemed to confirm what Leland had said about being nervous.

"Well, you seem to be in pretty decent shape," said Doctor Tom, later, at the desk in his office. He riffled through Leland's EKG and other test results. "You could stand to lose a few pounds and I'm still concerned about your blood pressure. Yet none of the other tests indicate any evidence of hypertension. Still, I'd like you to come back again in three months." He looked across his desk to see Leland gazing out the window. "Leland, are you listening to me?"

"Sure, of course. Sorry."

"All right then. I'll see you in three months." He rose from his desk.

Leland stood up as well. "Doctor Tom?" he said, voice unsteady. "I was just wondering—is my heart supposed to sound that way?"

The doctor squinted and stifled a smile. "What way?"

"The way it sounded today."

He leaned forward and put his hand on Leland's shoulder. "Yes, of course. Why?"

"Because it sounds, I don't know . . . disgusting."

Doctor Tom laughed and walked Leland to the door. "You think it sounds disgusting? You ought to *see* one. *Yeecch.*"

Leland had to admit that going to the doctor as a remedy to Madeline's unfaithfulness wasn't much help. Actually, it had made things worse. During the days that followed the physical, Leland was haunted by the sound of his heart. It was aurally etched in his memory centers, an ever-present sound bite. It hadn't helped that he had purchased a stethoscope at a medical supply store and was constantly monitoring the damn thing. He just couldn't believe that something inside him could sound so utterly grotesque. Later, simply by closing his inner ear with a half-swallow, he was sure he could hear the odious organ, lurching through goo, playing its lurid viscous ditty.

The sound sickened him at the most inopportune moments: driving I-696, the autobahn of Detroit, at his new favorite speed, eighty-five miles per hour; in the middle of a meeting, discussing the alleged importance of a new spiff program to his fellow salespeople; during one of his mother's meals, lovingly laden with saturated fats. (How could he tell her that he had lost his appetite because his wife was fooling around on him and the sound of his own heart made him want to puke? All that mattered was if Leland didn't eat, her week was ruined.)

Worse than all of them though, was when the sound sickened him in bed, with Madeline. Two repeats of Friday night's furtive coupling had occurred and Leland realized that their sex life had been staggeringly good since he had discovered her affair. She would come home late at night, wanting him, telling him that she wanted him. Of course, he still hadn't mentioned to her that he knew about her and her pesky paramour. He also knew that he shouldn't be having anything to do with her sexually. The thing was, Leland still loved her and he was, after all, a man. A weak man, apparently. So he would give in and it would be wonderful.

Mostly. The problem was near the end, with Madeline urging him on, saying his name again and again. (Yet another sound bite.) That time when a man's heart should be soaring, singing fast and low, at that time, all he could hear in his head was: *fluullggsha, fluullggsha, fluullggsha, fluullggsha* . . .

At the moment of climax, the noise of his heart also peaked—in his ears, in his chest cavity, along his carotid artery, through his wrists and ankles, in his temples. The sound invaded his physiognomy, took over. It was all he could hear, all he could think of, and it obliterated whatever pleasure he should have been feeling. Afterward, Madeline would fall immediately asleep. He was left wide-awake, with only his snoring, cuckolding spouse and a hideous heart to keep him company.

"Stop thinking about your heart, for Christ's sake," said Leland's mother, standing over him as he ate at her worn gold-speckled Formica kitchen table. "Just forget about it and let it do its job. You were always like this when you were little. Always getting all worked up over something you had no control over. Just stop it."

Leland let his head hang over his slab of rump roast. The gravy was already starting to congeal. "I know, Ma. But I can hear it. I can't sleep at night."

"No you can't hear it. You just think you can. It's all right here," she held the filed tip of her fingernail to her forehead. "Now I want you to forget about it. Do you hear me? Stop making yourself crazy, honey."

Leland watched a tiny red mark appear and then vanish on his mother's creased temple as she removed her finger.

"I will, Ma." He knew he wouldn't, couldn't. He hadn't told his mother about Madeline and her lover. It hadn't seemed like a good idea.

On the way home from his mother's, Leland listened to a new telephone tape for the first time in days. After listening to a few conversations of no interest, he changed his mind and put in an old T-Bone Walker cassette. Of course, all the songs were about betrayal—"Cold Hearted Woman," "Treat Me So Low Down"—so he had to turn it off. Leland made a mental note to not listen to the blues so much. Who the hell did he think he was anyway? He was a pasty white guy who lived in the suburbs, not the Mississippi Delta.

He put the phone tape back in and listened to two boring conversations of his own. On the next one, he recognized Jim's voice. The moment he heard it, it occurred to Leland that he could easily find out where Jim lived. He knew the phone number. (Leland had quietly installed Caller ID a while ago. Madeline didn't notice at this point or didn't care.) He could go over to Jim's house and talk to him. Or even kill him. Except Leland wasn't really the murdering type. (Another irony about his penchant for the blues.) He listened to the conversation. It was longer than usual and there was much more about him:

HIM: I'm looking forward to seeing you tonight.

HER: Me too.

HIM: Any problems getting away?

HER: No.

HIM: What is it?

HER: Oh, it's just that I'm starting to feel so bad about all this. Poor Leland really doesn't have a clue.

HIM: Starting? It's a little late for that. Don't you think?

HER: Shut up.

HIM: Why do you feel bad? You told me you yourself that you couldn't take any more of him. You two don't talk. He doesn't care about anything.

HER: I know. It's just, we've been . . .
HIM: What?
HER: Nothing. Just talking more.
HIM: Forget it. He doesn't deserve you.
HER: And you do?
HIM: Of course. I'll see you tonight.

Things were changing in Leland's favor. He could tell by her tone of voice. She felt bad, she had said it herself. Lover man, on the other hand, had a change of heart as well. He saw things falling apart for himself and attacked Leland. But Madeline defended him. Leland felt elated by all this, until he realized that she was with him right now.

That night, after collapsing into bed by himself shortly after nine, Leland awakened at 4:07 a.m. He'd been having an awful dream, but couldn't, for the life of him, remember it. There were so many other things to concentrate on: profuse sweating, loss of breath, intense free-floating terror, and of course, the abhorrent, chugging, gooshy organ inside his chest, splashing away, like someone trying to extricate himself from quicksand, just barely managing to stay above the surface.

Leland pounded at his chest, which really only made it worse. Plus, it hurt. He looked over at Madeline, who had apparently come in after he had gone to bed. She lay there, mouth open, snoring gently. How she could sleep the sleep of the guiltless, he did not know, but her face revealed no remorse. Leland thought about smothering her with a pillow, but knew he couldn't do it. No, the real problem was that his heart was making too much noise. He covered his ears. A bad idea. The sound grew louder, and he could hear his pulse as well. The two echoed in his skull, down his bones, all through his body, a disgusting tag-team of blurting blood. Leland pulled his fingers from his ears, sat up in bed, trying not to pant, wanting to calm down, succeeding only for a minute or two before the noise grew louder again. He got out of bed.

At first light, Madeline awoke to a strange sound. She found Leland lying on the floor of the living room, the television on loud, tuned to an empty channel where it emitted a high, frosty sound. He looked at her when she walked into the room, but didn't say anything.

"Leland, what's going on?" she asked, bending over him. "What are you doing?"

"I'm going to fix my lunch for work," said Leland, getting up. He walked out of the living room, down the hall, into the kitchen.

Madeline stood there for a moment, then turned off the television.

Every day for the next week, Leland fixed his lunch, went to work, came home, ate dinner, watched anything that was on television, went to bed. He didn't listen to any more of the tapes; he didn't go for any drives. Madeline went out on Tuesday and came home late, but no other nights. She seemed genuinely worried about Leland, but he didn't really notice. When she asked him something, he answered only yes or no.

Every night, after Leland went to bed, he would sleep for approximately five hours, then wake up at 4:07 a.m. or 4:09 a.m. When he awoke, it was to the ugly, mutating, impossible utterances of his heart—*fluorg* and *plaaceh* and sounds like them. They kept him walking around the house, hyperventilating or retching by the toilet until morning and its attendant distractions.

At dawn on Friday, after finding Leland on the floor of the living room, television blaring white noise, for the fifth day in a row, Madeline started screaming at him. "What is wrong, Leland? Why are you doing this? Why won't you tell me what's going on?"

Leland emptily viewed the molecules of light vibrating on the television screen. When he spoke, his voice was flat, with no coloration of tone or emphasis. "I don't like you fucking another man."

Madeline closed her eyes for a moment, expelled all the air from her lungs. When she opened her eyes again, Leland was still staring at the screen. She took a long breath, then walked over to the television and knelt in front of it.

"I'm not going to do it any more, Leland."

Leland said nothing, shifted his gaze to the clock. He had stilled its pendulum five days ago.

"All right?" she asked quietly, turning around to look at him.

Leland nodded.

After that, Madeline was home when she wasn't at work. She would come home right after work and stay with Leland all night. They ate casseroles or frozen dinners with big plates of salad. Madeline spoke to him about her day. Leland told her about what happened during his day and even smiled sometimes. Occasionally, they went to a restaurant on the weekends, a little Mexican place a few miles away. They started to have sex again, but it was nowhere near as good as it was when Madeline would come home late at night and wake Leland up.

What still woke Leland up every night was the sound of his heart. Now its clamorings reminded him of a toilet: short, repeated flushes. Except the bowl never filled and the flushing never stopped. Leland had learned to eat before bed so he would have something to vomit when he woke up. It was easier that way, avoiding the dry heaves. Madeline got up with him for the first few weeks when she heard him wheezing and sobbing in the living room; gradually she realized that he didn't really want her there. She would stand in the doorway of their bedroom for a moment listening to him, and then she would lie back down.

Every morning, she would suggest that he go see someone, a therapist, but he would always refuse, saying there was nothing anyone could do, no one could change a sound, alter the way it affected you, take it back so you could unhear it.

After a few weeks, Madeline started disappearing again, not bothering to call or even come home at all. Leland had been expecting this all along. He noticed that his heart now seemed louder than ever, that the muck inside him had grown deeper and stickier and filthier.

On the day Leland decided to silence his heart, he left work early and went to his mother's house. She was pleased that he had dropped by unexpectedly.

"You look pale," she said, touching his face. Then she made him dinner, a nice, extra-well-done pot roast with instant mashed potatoes. Leland ate as much of it as he could, which wasn't much. While she was cleaning up, he went upstairs. It was in an old early American chest of drawers that he found what he was looking for: his father's .38 police special and a half box of shells. He stashed them in a box of books, came back downstairs, and told his mother that he was going to take them home. She was always pleased to get rid of stuff from his old room. Leland gave his mother a hug, brushed his lips against her downy cheek, and told her that he had to go.

Their house was quiet when Leland got there. The windows were open, objects were missing from the living room and there was a note for him on the coffee table. He set the box down, took off his jacket and lay on the couch. He could hear his heart now, high and loud in his chest. He thought about what was in the box. He thought about opening it up, but he lay there instead.

At that moment, Leland noticed all the noise outside at this time of the evening: the traffic on Woodward Avenue; the faraway *burr* of a lawnmower; kids playing outside, their last harried attempts at play before the flickering of the street lights; and the susurrus of the wind through the trees, the low and tremulous sigh of leaves as they brushed together before falling.

For a long moment, Leland heard all that instead of his heart. When he realized what had happened, he heard his heart again, but now the sound no longer sickened him. Soon, it fell silent.

Leland got up from the couch, walked over to the box, picked up the gun, and unloaded it. He took all the shells out to the front of his house and dropped them one at a time down the sewer. He walked back into the house and lay again on the couch. Then Leland held a pillow tight to his chest and fell asleep to the rhythm of his breath.

downtown

I t was a big accident and I saw the whole thing. A semitrailer in front of me tried to turn the median too quickly. It was almost graceful really. The standard car accident slo-mo effect.

When it flipped, all these barrels flew out of the back, barrels breaking like dodo eggs on the concrete. Grainy brown sludge just gooshed out of them. I knew right away that it was cooking grease. There must have been hundreds of gallons. All the cars stopped and watched like it was some sort of natural wonder.

Then the smell.

I used to work at the Flaming Embers downtown and I know that smell. (Olfactory simulation: Drop a piece of meat behind a shelf, then "discover" it a week later.) It's what gets scraped off the grill. The corrupt remains of scared animal flesh. Yum.

By now, the stuff was oozing all over the street. I don't know how, but I could feel it around my tires, like soft dirt between my toes, like quicksand.

By the time the police arrived, the smell was about unbearable. I opened the door of my car to see how deep it was. Big mistake.

I threw up on the leg of a policeman. Then he threw up. I closed the door fast, then wiped my mouth with a tissue from my glove box.

I was trapped in a thin-shelled, rusting car.

I tried not to think about it, tried to forget what was there in front of me, all around me. I was breathing through a rag I found under my seat.

Finally, the cops started letting cars go. The one I ralphed on waved me through. I looked the other way and proceeded to the first car wash I could find.

Part 3

Men in blue uniforms squinted and exhaled as I approached. Some of them had on matching blue turbans. Don't ask me why, but Sikhs working in car washes are very common in Detroit. (Theory: perhaps turbans are good for drying those hard-to-reach places, like wheel wells?)

I jumped out and ran into the car wash building. I didn't even care if the workers stole the silver coins from the change compartment between the seats.

Inside, I watched through a long series of windows that just stretched on. I watched my car burst through suspended strips of dark rubber, brilliant daylight shooting through the chinks into the warm damp breath of the car wash. I watched the grease slide off my hubcaps as if they were hot frying pans. I knew the stink would never leave my car.

I walked over to the cashier counter. A teenage girl with blue hair and kabuki make-up looked through me. Next to the register was a stack of little pine tree car deodorizers, the useless kind you hang from your rearview mirror, overpriced at $2.69 each.

I bought two.

traffic reports

nothing to worry about. Just a little hole.

It is a small puncture on the driver's side roof panel about halfway up. Not a large hole by any means, even Bilner knows that. It is just a little hole. A cute little bullet hole. Nothing to worry about.

Bilner's friend, Al Kozikowski, who knows about these sorts of things, who actually carries a gun most of the time, says that it was probably from a .22. They are standing next to the car, in front of Al's apartment building. The late spring sky is a purple-blue, melting quickly into night.

"A pea shooter," Al says. "A deuce-deuce ain't shit from a moving car. I doubt that it would have killed you."

"Yeah, maybe it would have only gone through my eye," says Bilner. "Or severed my brain stem. You know, nothing serious."

"It was probably just some kids," Al says. "If they had wanted to hurt you, they could have, believe me."

"That's a real comfort." Bilner feels his eyelid start to twitch. "So should I report this or what?"

"You'll want to do it for your insurance. But it's not gonna make any difference unless you saw them, or you got a license number." Al pauses to pluck a mint from a small metal box. He pops it in his mouth and then looks at Bilner, who is obviously worried. "Look, I really wouldn't fret about this too much," he says. "The gun they used isn't all that dangerous. It's a plinker."

"A what?"

"A plinker. It's the sound a can makes when you shoot it, you know, like with a BB gun? Plink. Plink." When Al says *plink,* he raises his voice just slightly.

Then it occurs to Bilner. This whole thing isn't so bad. He hasn't really been shot at, only *plinked* at.

After Bilner leaves Al's place, he decides to report the incident to the police. Since it happened on I-75 near the McNichols exit, well within Detroit City limits, he heads for the Palmer Park precinct, which is only about a mile from Al's apartment. On the way there, he has to stop at a railroad crossing—one engine and at least a dozen cabooses huffing past. The wait makes him anxious again. Finally, the last caboose rolls by.

The police ask him questions, write down most of what he says. One of them even goes out to look at Bilner's car and comes back with a squished bullet. "Possibly a .22," he says to the other officer. They are much more interested than Bilner had anticipated. According to Al, police in that area weren't much help. They'd show up if you called about an armed robbery, but if your car was broken into, good luck. You wouldn't even see them. After it is all over, Bilner realizes that they *had* to be interested. Lately, there has been a lot of what the TV news calls "roadside shootings." That is, people shooting at other people on the expressways, from the overpasses, or most anywhere else on the street. Most of it takes place while driving in cars. It is a natural for Detroit.

At about 8:45 p.m., barely a half hour after he leaves the police station, Bilner gets a call. He is at home, in front of the television, trying to relax with the help of an extra large vodka, when the phone rings. A reporter from one of the local television stations wants to know if Bilner is going to be home and could they come by to ask him a few questions? Bilner is tired, and shaking a little, but he says all right.

"Is the car there?" the reporter asks cautiously, after getting directions to Bilner's house.

"Well yeah," says Bilner. "I have to drive it to work tomorrow."

"Great," the reporter says. *Click.*

Immediately after hanging up, Bilner gets two more calls from other TV stations and one from the *Detroit Free Press.* How do they all know about it so soon?

Bilner is good and numb by 11 p.m. He has been drinking before, during, and after his various interviews. Now it is time to see what he looks like on television. Since he does not really like watching the news, he watches the channel that is the most entertaining. His favorite station has a newscaster with a crazy big toupee that is a very different color from his real hair, which has been carefully lacquered and blended into the toupee, but still sticks out around his ears like bleached, blow-dried wheat. The chair from which he reads the news is always raised, like a kid's booster seat, so he seems taller than the other people on the show. Bilner has also heard about the newscaster getting in bar brawls or going on the air drunk. Sometimes he argues with the other people on the show, or during his famous editorials he might do something like challenge the mayor to a boxing match. This sort of thing happens regularly, so the station has the best ratings for news in town. Tonight, the newscaster's hair is all poufed up on one side like he had been caught in the wind. Bilner is one of the top stories.

"A suburban man never knew what hit him this evening, until he found out it was a bullet," is how the newscaster begins the story. He talks about the epidemic of freeway shootings and how we now have one more to add to the list. They go to the videotape—a shot of the area on the freeway where Bilner's car had been hit. "It happened right here around seven-fifteen this evening . . ." a disembodied voice said over the picture. "A shot fired at this car." The scene changes—Bilner's car in the driveway of Bilner's house. Then a close-up of the roof of his Mercury Grand Marquis and there was the hole! You can barely see it for all the light. The next shot is a bleached-out Bilner himself, talking to the albino reporter. Bilner feels the need to squint as he watches.

BILNER: I was driving along I-75 when I heard a pop and then a sort of metal-
    lic sound.
REPORTER: Did you get a look at the person or persons who shot at you? Could
    you make out anything? How many there were? Age? Race?
BILNER: I thought I hit a rock or something.
REPORTER: So you didn't see the shooter?
BILNER: No, I thought it was a rock.

Bilner looks like hell on television, all pasty and scared in the brightness, a paralyzed night animal right before the moment of impact, before it becomes an anonymous wad of fur and black blood, a pile of guts on the side of the road. He feels like a fool. Bilner quickly flips to one of the other channels and there he is again, washed-out and blinking, repeating the same inanities but with a different microphone in front of him.

After he watches himself, Bilner feels ill. He sits back on his couch and tries unsuccessfully to take a few deep breaths when the phone rings. It is someone from one of the local suburban newspapers. Again, Bilner goes through the details of his close call. No, he did not see what the person looked like, black or white, who shot at him. He had just heard a strange sound and when he pulled the car over to check, he saw the bullet hole. That was it. No, there was no one he could think of who would want to shoot at him. No more questions. Goodbye.

After he hangs up, the phone rings again immediately. It is Bilner's mother. "I saw you on the news," she says, her voice quavering, but also very loud over the phone, as usual. "Are you all right?"

"Yes Mother, I'm fine. Just go to bed. I'm perfectly okay."

"Are you sure? I was just watching TV and there you were. They said someone shot at you."

"It was just an accident, Mom. No harm done."

"Are you sure you're all right?"

"Yes, Mom. I'm sure."

"Those goddamn black bastards—"

"Goodnight, Mom."

After he hangs up, Bilner takes the receiver off its cradle and lays it on the table. As he heads upstairs, he hears the recorded voice of a woman saying "If you'd like to make a call, hang up and try again. If you need help, please . . ."

The next day at work, Bilner is a hero. There are people waiting for him, standing around his desk when he walks into the office. He is welcomed with a lot of warm "How are you's?" and reassuring pats on the shoulder. Even his boss is there, ruddy as ever, a lip of fat hanging over his starched white collar. He actually shakes Bilner's hand. Firmly, but not *too* firmly.

"Bilner, are you all right? I wasn't sure if you'd be in today after I saw you on the news last night. You must be pretty shook up."

"I'm okay, Mr. Hudson, really. The bullet didn't come anywhere near me."

The people around Bilner's desk are listening carefully to everything the boss says. "Still it must be horrifying to have someone take a random shot at you."

Bilner nods attentively as if he were in a sales meeting. *Yes. Random shot.*

The next week or so, business is great. All his accounts have seen him on the news and are full of support for him. His contact at Ford just keeps telling him how sorry he is that it happened. He then puts in a $20,000 order for dome light covers. This is the kind of sympathy Bilner can use.

The only problem is, Bilner is still having a hard time sleeping at night. It is starting to affect him. Three days after the incident, he is caught in a traffic jam on the Chrysler freeway on his way to an early appointment. He notices a dealer sticker on the trunk lid of the car in front of him. It reads: *HITMAN CADILLAC.*

Is this some sort of joke? If it is, he thinks, it isn't funny. Not the least bit. Finally, Bilner figures out that the sticker actually says: *WHITMAN CADIL-LAC.* The *W* is hidden within a large ornate crest. The whole thing is stupid, but it continues to upset him all that day.

He has also started to notice graffiti on the overpasses and median walls of the various expressways. Mostly it is gang names, stuff he does not under-stand, like: *FUD 667 Beyond Evil* or *God sent his only teeth.* But sometimes there are other things that kind of scare him. On the side of one overpass, someone sprayed: *I am here to whip people and whip them I shall.* The person had even signed a name to it: *Raven.*

The next day, there is another freeway shooting, this time on the Lodge. The victim is not as fortunate as Bilner. He is shot through the neck. The man, bleeding all over the place, drives himself to Henry Ford Hospital. By the time he finally gets there, he is barely conscious.

The newscaster: "Our freeways claim another victim. A three mile drive becomes a bloody journey for one man." He warns Bilner that the following footage may be too graphic for some people. "You might want to turn your head," he says. After that, Bilner *has* to look, but he is sorry that he does. The front seat of the man's car is sodden with blood. Bilner sees it beaded up and smeared on the dashboard.

After the footage of the car, the newscaster puts his script aside and makes what appears to be an improvised, impassioned plea. "We must stop this madness," he says. "It must end today . . . *now.*" Then the newscaster lets out a small, barely audible burp.

One morning the next week, Bilner notices a woman in another car holding a sandy-colored teddy bear on her lap. At a stoplight, he sees a Pontiac with so many religious medals and statues on the dashboard, Bilner wonders how the man can see through his windshield. Then there is another car, a Nissan, with its windows tinted so darkly Bilner can't even see an outline of a driver. At first, this seems like a good idea, but then Bilner starts to think that maybe only people who shoot at other cars would want such dark windows, so no one can see the guns. Bilner speeds up, hearing the repetitive *whomp* of bass tones emanating from the car as he passes.

At work, the novelty of Bilner's close call starts to fade. On Wednesday, a buyer cancels lunch at the last minute. Still, there is plenty of paper work to take care of, and that night it is almost seven thirty when Bilner leaves the office. He is supposed to be at a friend's house in Southfield by seven. By the time Bilner hits the Lodge, it is completely dark outside. Of course, it is always somewhat dark on this particular freeway, no matter what time of day. The Lodge: subterranean lanes pressed between fifty-foot ferroconcrete walls; glancing right angles of corroded girders and blanched exit signs; a strip of dim sky hanging overhead, the claustrophobic's view from inside the maze. Bilner wonders if he will receive a food pellet if he gets off at the correct exit.

On the wall of the Livernois overpass, there is a long message from

Raven: *The punishment is as just as it is inevitable.* Another confusing, threatening message. He should spell his name with an *i,* thinks Bilner.

Bilner is playing around with the radio (reception is often poor on the Lodge) when he notices a car in the middle lane coming up very fast, too fast, on his left. Suddenly, Bilner feels a sickness move through his upper torso, squeeze the breath from his lungs. There is a catch in his throat and without even thinking, Bilner turns his head sharply to the left to look at the person passing him. The person in the other car, a black man, turns his head at the same moment to look at Bilner. Their eyes meet through the glass and Bilner realizes that they are both waiting for the other to aim a gun. They drive in tandem for a long moment, each recognizing the terror in the other's eyes. Finally, Bilner hits the brakes. The other man speeds off, while Bilner pulls over to the side of the road to catch his breath. He sits in his car, panting, listening to his heart *thomp—thomp—thomp,* knowing there was nothing to be afraid of, but terrified anyway. A sliver of moon rises along the right side of his windshield. He does not sit there very long.

The next evening, Bilner is over at Al's apartment having an after-work drink. He does not tell Al about what happened the night before, but he has been thinking about it all day at work. Al puts a John Coltrane disc on the stereo and right in the middle of "Aisha," during one of the most lullingly beautiful parts, Bilner turns to Al and says, "How do I go about getting a gun?"

Al is a little surprised by this. He is a lot surprised. In fact, he has always suspected that Bilner never really approved of him carrying a gun. Of course, Bilner lives in the suburbs. "I think you're still upset about your little incident the other day," Al says.

"No, I'm fine about that, really."

Al looks skeptically at Bilner and keeps looking. Suddenly, Bilner feels the urge to talk more. "Well, I mean, certainly, it changed me. How could it not?

I mean, someone took a shot at me."

"They shot at your car. Remember, if they had wanted to shoot you, they could have very easily. Even then—"

"I know. *Plink, plink.* But it was still a gun. And I don't see any reason why I shouldn't have one."

"If you had had a gun, there still wouldn't have been anything you could have done about it."

Bilner takes a shallow breath. "I know."

"Have you ever even shot a gun before?"

"Sure I have. I mean, it's been a while."

"When?"

Bilner hesitates for a moment. "When I was in Boy Scouts."

Al smiles. "So the last time you shot a gun, you were like eleven years old?"

"Hey, I was good at it."

Al takes a sip from his glass of cabernet. From where Bilner is sitting, he can see where a drop has dried red on the rim. Al puts the glass down and starts to laugh. "That's great. And now you want to start carrying a gun around illegally."

"Wait. Don't you have permits for your guns?"

"Sure I do—to own them. But not to carry them around like I do."

"Oh. Well, I'm still interested."

Al picks up the wine glass again. "Hm. I think you should come to the range with me a couple of times. Then we'll see."

"Sure, whatever."

Bilner picks up his bottle of Molson and holds it out in front of him. "Well, hey. Here's to the right to bear arms."

Al takes a sip of his wine and frowns.

Their last trip to the range is when Al mentions that he can get Bilner anything he wants, no problem, all completely legal. Bilner does not ask questions when Al tells him that they will need to go over to Al's father's house. Bilner is just happy to hear that he can deal with someone he sort of knows. Still, it is kind of strange going over to some person's home to order a gun, as if it were Tupperware.

Mr. Kozikowski lives in an older area, on the northeast side of the city. Driving down his street, Bilner spots a white bungalow with some of the windows broken out. Someone has sprayed *CRACK HOUSE* in red paint on the aluminum siding. They pass another burned-out house that has been painted bright orange from top to bottom.

Mr. Kozikowski's place is about five houses down. It has bars on the windows and ornate protective grating designed to look like wrought iron on all the doors. Walking up, Bilner notices an old but intricate-looking burglar alarm system. The place is a fortress. Bilner wishes that he could do something like this with his car, or better yet, his person.

Most of the time that Bilner is there, Mr. Kozikowski just sits, inhaling oxygen from a tank next to his La-Z-Boy, nodding as Al points out guns from the catalog. When Mr. Kozikowski speaks, it is in short, splintered sentences—a harsh voice, full of phlegm. "I don't buy for too—many people these days," he says, reaching for his oxygen.

"I know. That's why I appreciate this, Mr. Kozikowski."

"My pleasure. I can't get out to the range—" Breath of oxygen. "—much these days. So this is fun for me."

After they page through the catalogs and magazines, Al gets out all of his father's guns. Bilner can't quite figure out why one immobile sixty-four-year-old man needs eleven guns, but he has them and this is how Bilner gets to see a Sig/Sauer, a Glock, a .38 police special, and a beautiful stainless Walther PPK/S.

"You look like a Walther man," Mr. Kozikowski says, when Bilner leans over to look at the gun. It is a corny thing to say, but somehow it seems all right coming from this older man.

"Thanks," says Bilner.

"I'll let you take a better look at it," Mr. Kozikowski says, picking up the gun. He ejects the magazine, pulls the slide back, checks the chamber, and hands it to Bilner.

The gun feels good. It fits Bilner's hand.

"Only 23 ounces," Al says.

Bilner is handling it gently, but now he grabs the gun fully and holds it out in front of him.

"The clip holds seven rounds. Pretty handy in case of an emergency," says Mr. Kozikowski.

"That's the only time you need it," Bilner says. This seems like the strong thing to say. He feels like maybe he is getting the hang of all this.

Mr. Kozikowski takes an extra deep drag of oxygen. "Damn right," he says.

It is not long before the shot fired at Bilner's car is forgotten. At least by everyone but Bilner. And possibly the people who deface the overpasses on his route to work. Near the McNichols exit on I-75, where it happened, someone has sprayed *head down*. Another one, closer to downtown, reads: *Incoming*. Raven is still at it too. Bilner spots the message near the Davison interchange: *Nothing is forbidden, All is permitted*.

At least he has survived everything—the shooting, the TV exposure, the ups and downs at work. Plus, he has his gun now and somehow it makes him feel different about things. He can defend himself. Of course, Al warned him that this might happen, that he might feel bigger and badder than everybody else for a while.

"You'll get over that," he said. "You better, 'cause it will just get you in trouble. The idea is to just live with the gun, get used to it. Don't be in love with it, but don't be afraid of it either."

As a gift, Al gave Bilner a small nylon holster to clip inside the waistband of his pants. Al showed him how to wear his shirt so the bulge of the gun was hardly noticeable. It felt a little strange, but exciting. Obviously, he can't carry the gun at work, so Bilner keeps it with the holster in the glove compartment of his car. Al has told him to get an alarm system, but he just hasn't gotten around to it yet.

So far, the only real stupid thing Bilner has done with the gun is referring to it as "his piece" in front of Al. His friend gave him an exasperated look and said, "Don't call it that." Al told him not even to refer to it in public. When he wanted to know if Bilner had the gun with him, Al would say, "You got your American Express?" (It took Bilner a while to figure out this code phrase. Finally, he remembered the old slogan: "Don't leave home without it.") At first, this had all seemed a bit silly, but Bilner dared not question it. Now when Al asks about the credit card, Bilner gives an almost imperceptible nod, the kind he has seen black men exchange when they pass each other on the street.

There is another shooting. It isn't on a freeway, or even within the city limits. It is on a surface street in one of Detroit's affluent suburbs. The media makes a big fuss about it. Bilner sees Al on the day it happens. "What they're saying on the news is nuts," Al says. "It's not related to the freeway shootings at all. They assassinated the guy. He just happened to be in his car at the time."

Bilner has to agree. It is not some haphazard shooting like his. Two men pull up next to another man sitting in a Lincoln Town Car at a traffic light. They shoot him nine times through the window of his car.

"Looks like the mob to me," Bilner says.

"Too messy. Probably drug related," says Al.

Bilner wonders if he will now be privy to inside information as a new member of the gun-toting public.

"Everyone's just upset 'cause it happened out there in the Vanilla Suburbs," Al continues. "Not a problem when it happens here in Chocolate City." This is Al's favorite way to describe the Metropolitan Detroit area.

Sure enough, Al is right. On the news that night, the suburban shooting is a much larger story than Bilner's measly random gunfire or even the man who had gotten shot in the neck. (Whom Bilner had found out was black.) There is a full five minutes of details about the "grisly roadside shooting in one of our suburbs." Lots of footage of the car, the stained, perforated interior, and the residential area in which it occurred—tidy Cape Cod houses with well-manicured front yards.

Behind the reporter during the film report, where Bilner is used to seeing young black kids waving and mugging for the camera at the scene of a hideous crime in the city, he is looking at impeccably groomed white people in tailored suits, bright polo shirts, and chinos, turning from the camera, their faces numbed and aghast.

When they cut back to the studio, Bilner's favorite newscaster talks on about what a tragedy it is, how no area is exempt, how we all are the cruel game of the roadside killers of our streets and freeways. Bilner notes that tonight his toupee is crooked and sticking out a little on one side. He is wearing it like a beret.

The newscaster stops for a moment, puts aside his script and looks directly into the camera. "I'll tell you something, folks. This really makes me mad. Some sicko waltzes into my home town and blows someone away right on the street." Bilner hears a noise off camera, a pencil falling on something metal.

"Well, I have something to say to you, Mr. Sicko." Bilner sits back in his chair and smiles. "What I have to say is this." The newscaster then pulls out what looks to be a .357 Magnum and lays it on the news desk. "I better not ever see you in *my* neighborhood."

There is more background noise in the newsroom. People rustling around, whispers, then a *thunk*. The newscaster stares at the camera. Bilner wonders if they will stop the broadcast, but then the newscaster says, "Now here's Dayna with the weather." Bilner turns off the television and heads up to bed.

Bilner has a rough time at work the next week. Companies just aren't buying his little plastic parts. After work on Thursday, he doesn't feel like going home, so he convinces some people from work to meet for drinks at a brewery down by the riverfront. When Bilner gets to the bar, there are only a few people from work. Nonetheless, they drink many pitchers of beer. Bilner and another person stay until two o'clock, when the bar closes.

When Bilner gets in his car, he realizes that he is drunker than he thought. Instead of getting on Jefferson Avenue right away where there might be police, he turns down Franklin Street and drives between the darkened warehouses, aiming his car toward the brightness of the Renaissance Center about a mile ahead. This will give him a chance to get some fresh air in his lungs and sober up.

The street is empty, but in front of him there is a car leading the way, radio blasting hip-hop—bass turned up all the way. Bilner can almost feel the pulsations in his car as they turn down Riopelle. In the song, a siren keeps repeating, puncturing the beat in a way that disturbs Bilner. In the back seat of the car, there is a dog with its head out the window, barking at strange intervals, with a regularity that has nothing to do with the thump-beat of the music, but with some secret internal animal rhythm. Perhaps the noise is directed toward something, but Bilner has no idea what it is. The dog is just barking into the air, at whatever *could* be there.

At Jefferson Avenue, the car with the dog turns right. Bilner turns left and drives about a quarter-mile to l-75. Along the ramp leading to the freeway a small cardboard sign staked in the dirt says: *CLOWN for your child's party.*

The freeway is almost deserted, and there are many stretches where the streetlights are out. This happens sometimes in the city. Long spans of the grid are just inexplicably dark. Bilner actually likes it when this occurs. He feels safer, less of a sitting duck for any crazies out there. He drives on for a few miles, passes the Mack exit, then the Church of Saint Josaphat, which faces the expressway.

Bilner moves over to the far right lane to be as inconspicuous as possible. There is only one other car behind him. By the configuration of the headlights in his rearview mirror, Bilner can tell that it is an old Chevrolet—mideighties. This is a talent he has had since childhood, one that always amuses the people who drive with him. The car moves closer. Bilner looks at the clock on his dash. He is surprised there aren't more barflies going home at 2:18 a.m. On the Warren Avenue overpass, near the university, there is a new message from Raven. It says: *The Horror.* Then beneath it, in a different color, *Da Ho.* Can't the guy just write *Fuck* on walls like everyone else?

A Mitsubishi gets on and drives in front of Bilner for a mile or so, then exits at West Grand Boulevard. In his rearview mirror, Bilner watches the Chevrolet move closer behind him, then pull up into the middle lane. This is nothing strange. What *is* strange is when the Chevrolet falls back a few car lengths as if to decide what to do next—then speeds up and falls back again. This is when Bilner opens the glove box. The Holbrook exit is coming up fast and he almost steers the car toward it, but instead, Bilner moves the maps out of the way, pulls the Walther out of its holster, and sets it on the seat next to him.

Bilner keeps checking his mirror. The Chevrolet falls back slightly, so he presses the accelerator until he is going seventy-three miles per hour. The

Chevy stays with him, about five car lengths behind. Bilner is having a hard time swallowing. There is a booming in his ears—a deep echo of blood and bone thumping in his head. The Chevrolet moves closer again, directly behind him this time. The freeway is still dark, but there is some ambient light from the surrounding surface streets, and Bilner thinks that maybe he sees four or five people in the car—a gang? They move over to the middle lane again and pull up slowly, intentionally moving into Bilner's blind spot.

He doesn't dare turn and look at them. For one thing, they will know he is scared and that might make them act. Also, Bilner does not want to turn face-first into a bullet. In his side-view mirror, he can now see the front fender of the Chevrolet. There is something trickling behind his right ear. He tries accelerating again and then slowing down. Each time, the Chevrolet moves with him. Bilner transfers the gun to his lap, pushes the safety off. He wipes his palm on his pants and looks down for a moment. There is a wet smear on the fabric next to the gun.

The Chevrolet starts inching up, expanding in Bilner's mirror. He cannot believe that this is happening again. Bilner finally turns for a moment to look at the front passenger window of the Chevy. In the darkness, he sees someone bending down, reaching for something on the floor of the car. Bilner grabs the gun and pushes down hard on the brakes. The Chevrolet veers close to his car. Bilner points the gun out his window, keeps his left hand low on the steering wheel and leans his head and shoulders down as far as he can on the passenger side. Bilner hears yelling, confused young voices. The Chevrolet veers closer to him, hits his car. There is a jolt, and Bilner feels the gun release in his hand.

The shot is loud, sending a wave of piercing sound through the car. Still crouched to the side, Bilner can see part of the roof of the Chevrolet. The car swerves far left, over the narrow shoulder, and scrapes the cement barrier in the middle of the freeway. He hears more screaming, then lifts his head and realizes what has happened. Even in the dark, Bilner sees something bulbous, almost glowing in the passenger window. Then hands reaching frantically, the fumbling glint of a belt buckle, and finally, jeans pulled back over naked buttocks.

Ahead of Bilner, the Chevrolet swerves again to the left, then straightens itself out. There is a strained, high-pitched *whoosh* as the car moves farther from him. Soon it is just a hum, a whisper of white noise that seems to sustain, even after the car is out of his view. Bilner puts the gun down on the seat and gets off at the next exit. He heads home the long way, the quiet way, through the city.

process

When I get to my parents' house this Sunday, I am surprised to hear that my father has locked himself in the basement.

Actually, that's just my mother's way of putting it. He is simply down in his darkroom and won't come up.

My father is a retired photographer. He worked for the electric company here in Detroit for thirty-four years, taking photographs of corporate bigwigs, nuclear power plants, "Live Better Electrically" model homes, retirement banquets, victims of electrocution. I have not seen him take any photographs lately. I have not seen him near a camera lately, except to show me one that he was planning to sell, even that was a few months ago. This is from a man who, during my childhood, was rarely seen without a camera. My elder sister and I were constantly being photographed. It was like a joke to us, the father's aberration from the child's eye. My sister used it to seem older to her friends, to create the illusion of maturity. "Oh, that's just my father," she would say. "He's always taking pictures of *something*." But in fact, he was.

Today, when I go downstairs to investigate, I find my father sitting at the hinge-top desk in his darkroom surrounded by black-and-white and color photographs of all configurations. On the adjacent table, there are at least ten or twelve separate stacks of photographs. All the lights are on in the small narrow room, except for the amber scoops, which hang over the processing area. Most of the equipment has been boxed, the long counter for all the chemicals and trays covered by a hard shiny cloth. On the wall above the counter, there is a plastic kitchen clock, its hands stopped at 11:36.

I say hello to my father. He looks up from a stack of curled 8 x 10s and smiles as if he had been expecting me any time now. "Why don't you come on upstairs and have a cup of tea with Mom and me?" I suggest.

"I can't right now," he says. "I'm too busy."

"Come on, it can wait." While I say this, my father gets up slowly, painfully from his chair and walks over to the built-in file cabinet. He pulls out a long drawer from the wall. I can't help but to think of a morgue. He takes from the drawer a thick bundle of photos held together with a crumbling rubber band, puts it on his desk, and carefully sits back down.

I lean over my father's shoulder to get a closer look at the photograph on the top of the bundle. It is a reddish color shot from the late sixties (I estimate). In the photo, all my maternal aunts and uncles are in the kitchen of a cottage in Ontario owned by my late grandparents. The table is full of luncheon food: Wonder bread, Velvet peanut butter, slices of ham and salami. My Uncle Phil is pulling back the tines of a fork as if he is about to blast my Aunt Agnes with potato salad. All my aunts and uncles are laughing. My mother is sitting quietly off to one side, smiling almost beatifically. She is far enough away from the table and I can see that she is pregnant, presumably with me.

I look over at one of the other stacks on the table next to my father's desk. There is a photograph of my mother, my sister, and me at a canyon somewhere in Utah, early-seventies. On the pile next to it, a portrait of my father's brothers and sisters, all darkly dressed in their Sunday clothes. My father, of course, is not in any of these.

"Come on. Go on up and talk to your mother," my father says. "I'll be up in a little while. Go on, scoot."

Upstairs, my mother and I sit at the kitchen table waiting for the water for our tea to boil. On my mother's side of the table is a brilliant quivering patch of sunlight, a rectangle formed by the window over the sink. Studying it, I realize how much dust there is in the air at my parents' house. Outside, a cloud goes past the sun and the patch almost disappears. In the dimness, I look over at my mother. She is leaning back in her chair, her head not quite touching the wall. Against the floral wallpaper, she looks tired. Her white pepper hair is dirty and lank. She rubs her hands as she talks to me.

"He's been this way all weekend," she says. "Friday morning, he got up and went straight down there. He hasn't been upstairs since, except to eat, sleep, and go to the bathroom."

The water starts to boil. I get up to take the kettle off the burner. "What's he going to do with all those photographs?" I ask.

"He told me he's going to give them away. And when I asked him why, he said *Why not?*"

I flick the knob to off. "Who's he going to give them to?"

"He's making piles for all your aunts and uncles, all that are left. He's got pictures of all your cousins from the time they were babies to when they graduated from college."

"And pictures of their babies, too."

"And he would have some of yours too, if you had any."

I pour two cups of hot water. Near the stove, there is a plastic container where my mother keeps the tea. I pull out a single bag and drop it into the first cup. After a few seconds, the water darkens and I plunge it into the other cup.

My mother and I drink our tea. We discuss my life, how I am doing at my job, who I am seeing, things like that. She tells me how my sister is getting along with her husband and two children. We talk about what we always talk about. It doesn't really feel all that different without my father there. Often when I visit, he just sits in his chair in the adjoining room (the family room). My mother and I talk while he reads the newspaper, entering the conversation only now and then.

Soon enough, my mother starts to fill me in on which friends of hers have which illnesses. My mother is getting to this age. After a while, I can take no more of hearing about who is dead, who is dying, and who is merely miserable. I tell my mother that I am going to go back downstairs to check on Dad, make sure he is okay.

My parents' basement is divided into two halves. The right side is the television room: light oak paneling, beige thick pile carpeting, dropped acoustical tile ceiling. The furniture is my parents' first living room set from the fifties.

The left side is the utility area. It is dark and untiled and hidden behind a curtain of dense fabric displaying giant faded pink orchids, pointed tongues on a pattern of gray and green stems. On this side, there is no ceiling really, only naked wood, the unvarnished belly of the first floor. Wires and cables run straight through two-by-fours and lead to sockets with bare bulbs that, when they are on, give off a harsh stripped-down light. A cord hangs from a socket down to a dehumidifier. There is a low-pitched hum as I walk past.

Ahead, my parents' furnace is outlined only by its own pilot light, glowing behind the ribbed iron door. Mottled and rusty tentacles reach up and clutch the floor above. As a small child, I was terrified of this furnace. The whoosh of its hot breath would wake me in the middle of the night, remind me of the presence of something awful, keep me wide-eyed with an erratic tone song of pings and pocks. Even as I got to be nine, ten years old, it still bothered me to walk past.

Today, I feel some of the old chill as I walk past the furnace, toward my father's darkroom. I hasten my step just a little, as if not to acknowledge it.

When I enter the darkroom, my father is still sorting photographs. He has cabinets full of them, overflowing with them. He is a man who took photographs for the sheer pleasure of the act, with no thought as to where he would put them all. He is now slouched over his desk, shoulder deep. I can see only his head moving above the stacks.

He has not yet noticed me and I stand there looking at the piles of photographs on the table next to him. By looking at the top photos, I can guess which stacks are for which people. But there is one pile that has nothing I recognize.

"Whose stack is this?" I ask.

My father looks up, unsurprised, and sits back straight in his chair. He folds his arms. "I don't really know," he says.

I pick up the stack and start looking through it. I have never seen these photographs before. There are about seventy 8 x 10s, all black-and-white. Judging from the cars I see, they appear to be mostly from the sixties. Here are some of the pictures I see:

— A downtown pawnshop, at night, with its front door open. An old man is at the doorway, staring harshly into the darkness, at the person taking the photograph.

— Women seated behind huge sewing machines, putting together the seats for automobiles.

— A drunk man, outside a nightclub called Frank Gagen's, passed out on the gleaming hood of a black Cadillac.

— Men waiting in line, at dusk, in front of the old Capitol Burlesk on Woodward, hats pulled down, looking away.

— A bright-faced young black man polishing a hubcap at a car wash called Paul's Wash-O-Mat.

My father leans over and glances at the photo of the hubcap polisher. "I won a Freedom Foundation Award for that photograph," he says.

This is news to me. I did not know that my father won awards for anything.

"It was part of an exhibition in Washington. I got my name in the *Free Press* for it too," he says, tapping the photo with the side of his index finger. He smiles tentatively.

"I won the year before that, too." He flips through the stack that I hold in my hands, pulls out another photo and places it on the top. "For this one," he says. "They were both part of a work series I did."

The photograph reminds me a little of the Farm Security Administration work I had seen years ago, while up at college. There are two men standing, looking out from the overhead door of a barn. The sun is low; it is apparently late afternoon. Both men are dressed in jeans, one is wearing a T-shirt, the other a dark work shirt. I recognize the man in the T-shirt. It is my Uncle Steve, round-faced cowboy and small-time operator, the only one in the family who really broke away from the pattern. Beside him is a gaunt older man whom I do not recognize. But because of him, the photograph becomes almost a study in textures: the rough-hewn whitewashed wood of the barn; the stained soft contours of the man's work shirt, heavy with sweat; the face, creased and weather-beaten, dark with dust and sun. There is a quirk to the photo, too. The older man is not wearing a cowboy hat like my uncle, but sports a fedora tilted rakishly to the right.

Both men look winded, as if they have just finished some strenuous job. Across the doorway, there is a metal bar, which my uncle leans on with both hands. He is looking off to the side, somewhere I do not know. The older man is staring straight ahead, one leathery hand clasping the bar, the other holding a cigarette. On the border of the photograph is a small caption in faded ink that reads: *The Work Before Day's End.*

My father reaches over and gently takes the stack of photos from my hands and puts them back in their place on the table.

"Why didn't you ever show me those before?" I ask.

"I don't know. I guess by the time you got old enough to appreciate that sort of thing, I hadn't done it for years. There didn't seem to be much point to it." He picks up a large stack and hands it to me. "Here," he says. "This is yours. It's not quite done. I haven't gotten to when you were a baby yet."

On the top of the stack is a 5 x 7 taken when I was about four years old. My sister is in it too. She is wearing a Halloween monster mask and holding her hands out as if to grab me. I am screaming hysterically.

Farther down in the pile, I am eight years old, in my wagon, hurling down the driveway of our house.

At thirteen, building a model car, sitting at the very desk (covered with newspapers) that my father is sitting at right now.

Eighteen—A color photograph. I am in my graduation gown, in my room. Behind me, over my right shoulder, there is a long strip of black. Earlier that year, I had convinced my parents to let me paint one wall of my room flat black. It is now the overpowering center of the photo.

Twenty-one—Leaving for senior year in college. I am with a friend, but I look anxious, ready to go.

I flip past the next ten years. There is a photo from last fall, at the cottage in Canada. Lake Saint Clair is behind me and it seems to stretch on and on, until the line between sky and water is indistinguishable. After this, there is a photograph from the same day. A close-up of my mother and father taken by me. They are holding each other and smiling. I have never seen this picture.

I flip to the last photograph in the pile. It is brownish and faded, not really a photograph at all. Images are hardly visible. A word chokes in my throat as I show it to my father.

"Hmmh," he grunts. "Chemicals." He takes it, tosses it into the now overflowing wastebasket.

Suddenly, I am annoyed by all this. I am tired of my father playing games, locking himself down here, not coming upstairs, not talking to my mother. I am tired of standing here. "What's going on, Dad?" I say. "Why are you doing this?"

My father looks up at me, smiling at the spark in my voice. He picks up his magnifying glass again and examines a black-and-white photograph that, oddly enough, is of him. He is leaning on a parking meter with the city behind him, circa 1970. "I guess I just got it into my head to clean up down here."

"Why now, all of a sudden?" I fold my arms.

"It's just time."

My father is bent over the desk, now looking carefully at a picture of my mother. It is one I've seen many times before. A photograph taken on my parents' honeymoon in Saugatuck, Michigan. My twenty-six-year-old mother, with full and dark hair, is sitting on the porch of a cabin, looking pensively at a large pottery vase. Seeing it now, I realize it is one of my father's first awkward attempts at art.

"Mom's worried," I say.

"Your mother's always worried. That's why we got married. It's a good balance. She worries about the future and I prepare for it."

He puts the photo down and looks at me. I suppose I don't have a very pleasant expression on my face.

"It's okay," he says. "She's tougher than you think. Besides, she's used to me staying in the darkroom for long periods of time. You don't remember, but back when you and your sister were little, I'd come down just to get some peace and quiet."

"I remember," I say.

"I guess that wasn't too nice of me to leave you two with your mother, especially after she'd had the both of you all day, but she never seemed to mind. And there were some things I needed to work on then."

"These?" I say, pointing to the pile of photos that belong to no one in particular.

"Uh-huh. Or if I wasn't down here working, I was out on the street, shooting or just looking around." He tucks his magnifying glass back in its sheath and places it on a small shelf in the desk.

"What did you want to do?"

"I had it in my head to get published in *LIFE* magazine."

"Wow. Really?"

"I guess I wanted something big. I almost got in there, too. The funny thing was, it was a family-type photo." My father chuckles a little. "After all my work series and city series, the one that almost gets in is that one of your sister with the mask. I had just sent it in for the hell of it. But I know they considered it for publication because when it came back, it had a bunch of initials on the back, like a lot of people had seen it. Someone toward the end must have nixed it."

"You never tried again?"

"Sure I did. I just never seemed to get that close again," he says, starting to fidget. My father can't keep still for too long. He takes a small fine-haired brush and lightly flicks it over a negative. "I got a few things published here and there. The company magazine, *Golf Journal,* that sort of thing."

"Why did you stop?"

"I didn't mean to. We just got busy. I was getting a lot of overtime and we needed the money. We were trying to fix up the house, and one of you kids was always getting sick. I'd come home and I was too tired to do anything."

My father tilts the shade of his desk lamp up a little and holds the negative up toward the light. A feathery gray shadow falls over his eyes.

"Were you working at Tollman's studio then, too?" I ask, turning my head away from the light.

"Only around the holidays. Four hours a night developing January graduation photos." He flips the light back down and places the negative on top of an envelope. "God, some nights I was seeing the kids from those photographs in my dreams. By Christmas, I couldn't wait to get out of there. Do you remember that place at all?"

I nod. "Of course. You used to take me there at least a couple times a year on Saturdays."

"Boy, what a dump," my father says. He smiles, as if at his own private joke, then looks down and starts to go through yet another stack of photographs. I realize this is my signal that he must get back to work. But suddenly, I do not want to leave. I want to stay with my father and talk some more. I want him to tell me more about Tollman's, the dingy walk-down studio with its worn linoleum floors, clouded casement windows, darkroom radio tuned to WJR, broadcasting from "The Golden Tower of the Fisher Building" to a tiny amber-lit room. I want to tell him how much he taught me about the process from 8 x 10s of pimply Cass Tech graduates. How much I remember from watching him at the enlarger, introducing the smooth bare paper to an image for ten seconds, then with one fluid motion of his hand plunging it into the tray of Dektol, touching it every few seconds, always keeping the print moving, never letting it sit too long. Watching, looking for it now, as beginnings of images appear on the paper. Vague shadows, unrecognizable at first as anything, slowly turning to the edges of outlines, then outlines themselves. Now grays: light and dark moving, a living chiaroscuro. Details finally falling in, rapidly now, like the moments that make up a life.

My father does not want to talk anymore.

Upstairs, I get ready to leave. As I put on my jacket I reassure my mother, tell her everything will be fine. She smiles weakly and gives me what can only be called a knowing glance. I give her a kiss in the hallway and am just about to walk to the basement door to yell my goodbye, when I hear my father's slow heavy footsteps on the staircase. I look over at my mother.

When my father finally gets upstairs, he gives me a hug and tells me to drive carefully. I tell him I will. We all walk to the door together.

Outside, it is starting to get dark. I walk to the street and get in my car. As I start it up, I look over at my mother and father standing behind the screen door. The mesh gives them a gauzy, soft-edged appearance. And although my father is waving at me, he looks distracted. Even in the fading light, I can see that he is already thinking about going back downstairs, the work he has left to do, and a small, quiet room.

spelunkers

She had been to my Web site, *The Paris of the Midwest Is Crumbling* (DiggerDetroit.net), and dropped me an e-mail. Lots of times I don't answer these e-mails because what I do—you know, this breaking into abandoned buildings to explore and take photos, then write about the experience—it's pretty fucking illegal. That's why I don't use my real name. Anyway, she contacted me and asked if I ever took anyone else on my explorations. I told her no, because that's what I tell everyone. Someone's always writing me, wanting to do a ride-along. Hey, I don't know these people. For all I know, it could be someone from the city who wants to arrest me.

Just for the record, I do have a small crew, which always includes my old musician friend Martin K. (His band, Riot Generation!—seminal eighties Detroit punk.) He's a good person to have along because he's a fireplug, a hockey player, and often pissed off about something. When you radiate rage, people tend to stay away, I've found. He's the only person I know who actually carries a blackjack. Martin makes his own—sews the leather himself, delicately fills it with lead shot till the little belly is taut, stitches it up, then braids a handle for it. He's a real craftsman. They're quite lovely actually, almost objets d'art. Obviously, it's no match for a Glock, but the sight of it quiets down a hostile hobo right fast. Don't nobody want to taste one of Martin's homemade saps.

Another one of my usuals is Chip, who looks about as little like a "Chip" as he possibly could, which is why we call him that. He grew up in the old-money Grosse Pointes. I'm not going to tell you who his Grandma is, but she's a famous soul singer whom you'd recognize by the fact that she gets wider every year. (Great story that Chip will neither confirm nor deny: A piano tuner comes to the mansion to fix Grandma's grand piano, which is not working. He pulls apart the Yamaha's keyboard to find that everything is completely glued together with Cheeto dust! *Awesome.*) Chip doesn't favor her though. He's tall, willowy, mochachino, with a 'fro for days. He's also the most talented graphic designer and Web guru I know. He's why my Web site looks so badass. It ain't me, that's for sure. I just take the pictures of the fucked-up shit, he's the one who makes it look *uber*-urban, *echt*-industrial, proto-apocalyptic, rustbelt cool, or whatever the underground magazines who worship Detroit are calling us these days.

Anyway, like I said, when this woman Jenna e-mailed me, I blew her off at first. Then she wrote back. Then wrote back again. And again. She mocked me for being some sort of hipster elitist who wouldn't help a sister out. She had a class called "The Dialectics of Graffiti" or some such bullshit at the university downtown and she wanted to go into an abandoned building to check out and photograph the tags for her thesis. She said that if I didn't help her, she would just do it herself and if something happened to her, let it be on my head. I didn't know if she was messing with me or not, but I finally wrote back, told her she was a crazy bitch and maybe I'd help her, but we'd definitely have to meet first. She had chutzpah, I'll say that.

Cut to the Olympic Grill on Warren and Cass. She said it would be easy to recognize her. When I walked into the place, which is just a run-down little greasy Greek diner on the edges of the university, the place was full of students, but over on one side was a semi-geeky-looking woman in her thirties with frizzy red hair bunched up on one side, freckles, and big chunky brown glasses. All she needed was braces and a "Kick Me" sign taped on her back to complete the look. She was holding up a sheet of paper with my *nom du web* on it: DIGGER.

"What the fuck are you doing?" I grabbed at the sheet, but she held it up over her head so I couldn't reach it. I winced a little at the sight of her inner arms, where the line of freckles seemed to recede into skin the color of butter pecan ice cream.

"Would you put that *down*," I said, getting pissed off fast.

Finally, she realized that I was serious and lowered the sign. I snatched it from her. She looked hurt. "What's the big deal?" she huffed.

"I could get arrested. There are people that don't like me and don't like what I do. I don't need to be identified to them so they can sock me in the nose."

She just laughed. As she did, her glasses slid down her tiny nose. She pushed them back into place with her index finger, a gesture that drives me crazy with its straight-up dorkiness. "What is so amusing?" I asked, getting more steamed by the moment.

"I don't know. *Sock in the nose*. It's just so old-fashionedy. It's funny."

I sat down in the booth and laid the sign face down on the table. "For someone who wants a favor, you're being a pain in the ass even sooner than I thought."

Her face fell into a pout. "I'm sorry."

I think she thought I'd be charmed by her high jinks. I'm afraid it takes more than this sort of thing to warm me up. But now she looked sad and I didn't like that either. When she sulked, her bottom lip divided into two plump sections. "It's okay," I said. "It's just that discretion is usually a good idea in these matters, okay?"

"Okay." She held out her hand. "I'm Jenna."

"Yeah, I figured."

She smiled at me, looking straight into my eyes for a long moment, which kind of creeped me out. I could tell she was skulking around in there, seeing if she could find anything there besides broken glass, curled flakes of infant brain-curdling lead-based paint, weathered plywood, an old shoe, and maybe a steaming heap of hobo poop. Truth was, I was hoping she would find something because now that she wasn't acting so loopy, I liked what I saw. What can I say? I have a thing for nerdy women.

We had coffee. "I need a guide," she said.

"Why me?"

"Your Web site is what got me hooked on the idea. You have that whole graffiti section. That's where I learned about Turtl and Eggs and Krakhed. I just figured if I wanted to go deeper, I'd need professional help."

"Those guys are over. Turtl's gone and the other guys have gone underground. Anyway, I'm not a professional. I don't know what I'm doing. You could get arrested."

She lifted a copper brow. "Have *you*?"

"No, but I'm just telling you. Sometimes the police are around. I've run into them."

"I'll take that chance. I'd really like to do this. I can handle myself. If anything happened, I wouldn't just be standing there screaming, like in the movies."

"Oh, you're going to wrestle the gun out of someone's hand?"

"There are guns?" The look on her face was priceless.

"I'm just messing with you."

"*Oh.*"

"Okay, now you're serious. That's better. You've seen the old United Artists Theatre on Bagley, right? The windows are almost completely covered with graffiti art."

"That sounds perfect. Where is it?"

"I can't believe you don't know about the place. It's an amazing old Charles Crane theater from the twenties. Didn't you do any research?"

I don't know why I was putting the screws to her. She went from smiling at me to looking pissed off. Her voice sharpened, then cracked. "Yeah, I did research."

"Doesn't sound like it. Where did you grow up?" This is the question that defines everyone in Detroit. Where you grew up is pretty much who you are, whether you like it or not.

She sighed. "Birmingham."

I tried to hide my smirk, but not really. "Slumming it, are we?"

She flicked my arm with her finger. "Shut up. Where did you grow up?"

"Westland."

"That's just as bad."

"No, it's not. People actually *work* in Westland. They drive Fords instead of BMWs and Mercedeses and Hummers."

That got her. "Know what *you* are?" she said. "You're a Detroit snob. *Ooh, I live in the city. I'm an Urban Pioneer. Look at me. I'm all street and shit.*"

"Is that what they say in *Burrming-ham*?" I said, laying on the upper-crust lockjaw. "Do they think that it's *so interesting* that you're studying *ghetto art*?"

She shook her raised middle finger at me. "All you hipsters that live in the city are so self-righteous."

"Stop calling me that. I'm not a fucking hipster."

"Oh *please.* You're the worst kind of hipster. You're such a hipster, you don't even think you're a hipster. You're an 'I'm beyond *hip*-hipster.'"

I got up to leave. "Okay. I'm not helping you. Go fuck yourself."

She started laughing at me. *Laughing.*

"What?" I spat out the word with as much disdain as I could muster.

"Wow. You really hate that, don't you? That's so funny. You think it's so terrible to be a hipster."

"I think you may be retarded, lady."

"I'm just *messing* with you." She was trying not to laugh now.

I sat back down. I looked at her and then I started cracking up. I don't know why, but I did.

It was after we got up to leave that I saw she had a limp. Every step she took leaned her to one side with a kind of swagger. I didn't know what to say, so I ignored it. Then she ignored me ignoring it. But it was there.

Three days later, on Saturday afternoon, I met her at the Cass Café. I had given her instructions: comfortable thick-soled shoes, long pants, flashlight, camera, cell phone, ID, etc. She had followed most of them except she was wearing a tight, short-sleeved T-shirt, one with Fred Sanford's head on it above a caption that said: "You Big Dummy." I could see the straps from her bra underneath and tried to overlook the effect it had on me.

"Hey," I said. Watching her walk in made me realize something.

She flashed a half-smile at me as she sat down. I could see she was nervous. "Coffee?"

"No thanks."

"Hey, I have to ask you this. Are you going to be all right getting around? This could get kind of physical in places."

"You mean my leg?"

I nodded.

Steely gaze directed right between my eyes. "I'll be fine."

I had to ask. "Um, so how did that happen?"

I watched her jaw tighten. "A car accident when I was a teenager. Three girls in a car. I was in the back seat. My two friends weren't so lucky."

I didn't know what to say. I looked at her to try to connect in some way, but her eyes were closed for a moment. I was happy when Martin approached the table. He wore gray Dickies and a gray sweatshirt, like some gym teacher ninja. The handle of a sap peeked out from under his shirt.

"Hey scro," I said. "What up?"

He shrugged. "The usual. Slowly dying inside."

I nodded. Martin glanced over at Jenna, then back at me.

"This is Jenna." I turned to her. "Jenna. Martin."

She smiled faintly at him. "Hey."

I had told him we'd have a guest. I couldn't tell if he was annoyed. Martin was hard to read, even for me. Chip, who wasn't joining us today, liked to say that Martin was a riddle wrapped in an enigma wrapped in a paradox wrapped in a delicious flour tortilla.

We paid for our coffee and split. "Let's take the Soccer Mom," I said, gesturing to Martin's old Chevy Astro van. As we drove, Jenna was much quieter than the last time I had seen her. I sort of liked her this way. We parked the van a block away from the theater. There were a fair number of cars out. I wondered if there was a Tigers game today.

Out on Bagley, we walked beneath the old fifties green and orange streamline marquee that had replaced the original one from the twenties. Here and there, empty bulb sockets stared at us like rusted eyes. We passed the old ticket booth, which stood hollow. The weathered gray plywood that sealed the entrance was encrusted with posters for long-forgotten films and hip-hop discs. Over that, someone had painted giant pink polka dots. Probably an acolyte of Tyree Guyton, who on Heidelberg Street had painted polka dots on old buses, car hoods, trashed kitchen appliances, and a toothless block of abandoned houses—crazy vibrant splashes of color and life and energy in a neighborhood decimated by crack and blight—a ghetto theme park.

All these front doors were too conspicuous and too well sealed, so we walked around to the side. I scanned the streets. There was no one around, though I could hear whooping sport-o's a block away. We passed a doorway that someone had sealed with a sheet of plywood, tattooed with graffiti, and another Guyton-style painting of a round tan face with tiny infantine eyes and a single curl of hair rising up from the head. Someone had scrawled *Aorta* beneath it. Jenna stopped to take a photo. I looked at Martin. "How the hell did we get in?"

"We gotta do a little climbing."

"Oh fuck. I must have blocked that part. Where?"

"Down the way. I got directions from a tagger."

Jenna now looked really worried. Her eyes had widened and somehow her hair had gotten blown over from the side and was standing up all crazy-like. She reminded me of Buckwheat from the Little Rascals when he got scared. Except for the fact that she was, you know, so incredibly Caucasian.

I was a little hesitant to say something, but I thought I'd better. "You cool with that?"

She didn't seem so sure this time.

"Fuck it. Yes. I'll be okay."

I wasn't so sure I believed her.

"My dad would clobber me if he knew I was doing this," she said.

I nodded. "Yeah, mine too, but then he would have done it anyways."

Jenna looked at me in a weird way as I laughed. "Come on," I said.

For security's sake, I'm not going to get into too many details about how we got in, but suffice to say it was not pleasant. Walls were scaled and advice like "Whatever you do, don't look down" was dispensed, if that gives you some idea. But through it all, Jenna was fine.

Once we were in, there wasn't a lot of light, so both Martin and I had our Mag Lites trained on the floor ahead of us. Jenna was going to put hers on too, but I told her to save it. How much light did we need to illuminate trash, broken glass, giant molted flakes of paint, fast food boxes, and lots of old rags. Some tramp had a rag fetish. Before long, Jenna was taking it all in, limping along, utterly fascinated. I was amazed that she wasn't exhausted walking that way for so long, yet she wasn't. I paused as she pulled out her camera and photographed a partially open office door where light was seeping, glowing with dust motes. Someone had tagged the door: *Thru da eyes of syruz.*

I let Martin go explore up ahead. When the light got better, I got out my camera and started shooting random objects: a broken chair with half a metal film canister leaning against it, rumpled piles of clothes, a mosaic of shattered glass.

"Have you ever seen those pictures by Irving Penn?" Jenna asked. "The ones of the trash he found in the street?"

I stopped what I was doing and stared at her, stunned. "*Yeah.* I love those photographs. They're amazing. He made that stuff gorgeous."

"Have you seen that book of his? *Passage*?"

"I own it," I said, taking her hand. "Come on, we have to see the theater."

We caught up with Martin and let him lead the way. He walked us down a hallway covered with tags as Jenna snapped quick natural-light shots on the fly, mostly names: *Slack, Mo B, Mosh, Gray*, Mak.* People who wanted to be heard, to offer proof that they existed, but came to a deserted, broken place to do it. I don't know why that made sense to me, but it did.

We ended up in what was once the round inner lobby of the theater. The floors of the rotunda were covered with debris—paint and plaster, brick and statuary. You couldn't really say the walls were bare, because mostly there were no walls. Two of the three Gothic arches on one side of the rotunda were now stripped clean—the elements and the vandals were sloughing the place from the inside out, revealing the tessellated cinderblock bones of the building. Where there were walls, you could see remnants of gold-leafed ornamentation gone to chalk, traces of intricate designs, petroglyphs of former grandeur.

After more photographs, Martin kept us moving. It was a good thing that he truly seemed to know where he was going, because I for one was definitely distracted. I watched Jenna and could see a kind of terror and fascination in her ash-colored eyes as she scanned the carnage. But it changed when she saw me looking at her. *Busted.*

"You okay?" I asked, needing something to say, then thinking that I sounded too protective.

"This is incredible."

We went up a flight of side stairs. Somewhere beneath my feet, under the filth and curled paint and disintegrated plaster was softness, the vague memory of carpet. We surfaced onto the mezzanine for a full view of the theater from the back. Martin looked back at me. "The view's better from up here. And it's less dangerous."

Jenna walked up next to me. All of us stared out at an immense palace of ruin. Sunlight had indirectly found its way into the auditorium from ceiling fissures and smashed-out windows, giving the place a brownish gray cast. It was the color of the doves that I could hear roosting somewhere. The giant room smelled of damp and guano and rust and rotting plaster and moldering fabric, as if we had slalomed up the alimentary canal of some behemoth to its vast bloated stomach and were now examining what it had eaten before it died. Yet leaking in from somewhere above us was the high fresh smell of spring air.

Forty-foot-long tatters of curtains hung over what was once a stage. Flanking the stage were the jagged mammoth remnants of broken Gothic filigree where the pipe organs were housed. Above them, giant cone-shaped sconces snugged the ceiling. Traversing the sconces were X-shaped light vents now shattered or dissolved by water. On either side of the balcony were vestiges of what were once statues of long-gowned art deco Indian maidens. A small bas-relief of a face peeked at me from high, too far up for the vandals to smash.

"God," I said.

"Take a look at that proscenium," said Martin. "It's still incredible."

I felt how I always felt in these places: tranquil.

Next to me, Jenna was lost in wonderment, her moist bottom lip just slightly tipped open. "It's just so sad," she said to no one in particular. Then she raised her camera to her eye and scanned the great room as if she couldn't process the information in any other way. I knew how she felt. Sometimes real life was too intense for me to understand without a filter, a way to view it. I watched tears leak from beneath the viewfinder.

"It's so strange to think about the thousands of people—the millions—who walked through here over the years—seeing *Doctor Zhivago* or *I Am Curious (Yellow)* or *Shaft's Big Score* or whatever," I said. "Just standing here, you can tell that people laughed and cried and applauded here, smiled at each other. They threw popcorn and drank Pepsi and broke their teeth on Jujubes."

I felt stupid after I said it, but Jenna didn't laugh.

"It's beautiful," she said.

It stunned me that she should see it too. "I know. I don't know why. It's awful that this would ever happen to a building. This should never happen anywhere. But I see something like this and I want to try to find the beauty in it, make some sense of it, give it a reason, *fill* it with something."

Jenna turned to me, nodding. A tear flowed over her mouth, over the trace of a smile.

Martin looked at us both like we were fucking nuts.

Up in open high places I get that thing where you get the uncontrollable urge to jump? You can picture yourself jumping, maybe even hanging there in the air for a moment, legs wind-milling, an exemplar of cartoon physics. Poe wrote about it. He called it "The Imp of the Perverse." It sounds freaky to a lot of people, but anyone who's got it knows just what I'm talking about.

So I passed when Martin told us he was going up to the roof. Plus, this building is eighteen stories. He likes the exercise, but for me, that's a lot of climbing just to be terrified. Jenna and I headed up to the office floors to check the graffiti.

We had good luck on the first floor we stopped at. In one of the larger offices, almost everything had been painted. Sure, there were tags everywhere, but what interested me were the small murals on the windows—faces, hands, fish, animals, the sun, the moon, and other abstract objects that I couldn't always identify, in all the colors you could find in a can of *Krylon*. It was like standing in the middle of a Faberge egg. A big, fucked-up Faberge egg, mind you, but still incredible with the sun rushing in, glowing through the paint, tinting our faces and clothes, like photographs I'd seen of shows at the Fillmore in the sixties where the psychedelic lighting bathed everyone's dervishing, tripping bodies with color and design and madness. It made me feel that way being there with Jenna.

She was taking photographs left and right. "This is insane," she said. All at once, she seemed pleased and confused and astonished. "I've never seen anything like this."

I smiled at her. Maybe I was a cynical hipster, after all. Why was her excitement making me so strangely happy?

"Let me take your photograph," I said.

"Okay." She pushed up her glasses, tucked a longish strand of coppery frizz behind her ear.

I posed her standing between windows, taking care to get the light level right so you could see the faces painted on each of the windows—two Botero-style heads facing each other, eyes slitted blissfully, mouths agape in mutual moan, and her the unexpected third in the ménage. Lit from the sides, her face, ever so tilted, was surrounded by a corona of fire hair.

After I took the shot, I lowered the camera and looked at her. How long I did that, I do not know. She walked up to me, took my face in her hands. They were cool and smelled of dust and rusted iron and mint. I kissed her.

At the stairs, we ran into two gaunt, desperate-looking men dressed in stained, baggy clothes, on their way up. One of them had a long piece of copper pipe in his scarred-up hand. Crackheads rummaging for scrap metal.

I found myself unexpectedly shaken by the appearance of these two. They did not look friendly. I said "Hey" as they passed, not hostile, just acknowledgment. I could hear my own voice shake. It's never a good thing to sound scared, but I felt completely stripped of my usual armor of attitude. The one with the pipe stopped and eyed Jenna's camera. As I froze, there was a moment where I didn't really know what was going to happen. Then with a stomp of steel-toed brogan, Martin suddenly appeared above them, seventies Eastwood eyes burning holes into one crackhead, then the other. Without a word, they kept trudging up the stairs. Martin watched as they passed, hand resting on his stomach.

"You get up to the top already?" I asked, acting like nothing had just happened.

"I've been gone an hour, douche bag. Maybe you should turn your fucking cell on."

"Oh shit. I guess it was on vibrate."

He squinted over at Jenna, then at me. Disgusted, he shook his head.

That night, Jenna and I had dinner at Gandhi (chicken tikka, vegetable curry, papadams), and then we walked back to my place. She was surprised at how pretty my neighborhood is. I think she thought that I'd live in some stone ghetto. Actually, I live in a perfectly pleasant block of Hamtramck. (I didn't tell her that it is often referred to as "Birminghamtramck.") A nice Bangladeshi family with a bunch of kids lives one on side and some crazy messy Native Americans ("Red trash," as Chip calls them) on the other. The rest of the neighborhood is Hamtramck Melting Pot: black, Eastern European, Muslim, and what Jenna and her glossary of demeaning terms would call "Urban Pioneers."

"You know this area at all?" I said.

She nodded. "Actually, I do. My grandma on my Dad's side lived over by St. Florian. We used to go visit her when I was a kid."

"Did your dad grow up here?"

"No, they lived on the southwest side when he was growing up."

"Was it pretty tough then?"

She smirked. "To hear him tell it, it was."

We walked up to my porch. "Why did you smile when you said that?"

"He fancies himself kind of a tough guy."

"So," I said, "why's that funny?"

She looked at me and smirked again. "No reason."

We sat down on my glider. "My parents hated everything about Detroit," I said. "They moved from Detroit out to Westland right after the riots in '67 before I was even born. They never went into the city after that and they forbade me to go. My friends and I had to lie when we went to shows downtown."

Jenna looked at me in that sympathetic but not quite truly understanding way that I recognize. "Really?"

"Oh yeah. They hated Detroit. They were always saying *the goddamned niggers took over. They ruined the city. Goddamn sons-of-bitching jungle bun-*

nies. That goddamn jigaboo mayor. That sort of thing."

I watched Jenna wince at the words coming from my mouth. I was glad she was upset, but I didn't know why I was telling her all this. "That's pretty much what I grew up with," I said, trying to smile, but not really succeeding.

She exhaled, puffing her cheeks out. "They must love what you do now."

"Dad died a couple of years ago. We didn't talk for a long time after I first moved to the city. He never saw the Web site. But I think if the heart attack hadn't killed him, what I do now probably would have." I cleared my throat. "I would have been okay with that, by the way."

"How about your mom?"

"I talk to her once in a while. She's a little better now that Dad's gone."

"How do you mean better?"

"She doesn't hate everyone quite so much."

Jenna stayed over that night and never left. We saw each other pretty much constantly. That's kind of how I am. Chip likes to say that I go from zero to girlfriend in 2.4 seconds. That's true. I'll go for a year or two without anyone, like *no one*—then suddenly: *girlfriend.* I guess it's that way because I don't really date so much as just run into people. It's not the most efficient way to mate, I know, but I can't help it.

We settled into a domestic quiet that I wasn't exactly used to, but enjoyed. Jenna adapted to city living with only a few complaints—needing to be careful when you come in late, having to put locks and alarms on everything, the shaky infrastructure that means your garbage isn't always going to get picked up or the police may not show up when you call, Albanian gangstas, that sort of thing.

Still, everything was going fine except I hadn't posted anything on my Web site since she and I had hooked up. Jenna had pulled me away from my usual loneliness, which was what generally fueled my work. Thus my Internet public was complaining. Before I had nothing to do but enter abandoned buildings, take photos, go to the Burton Collection at the Main Library to research the history of those once grand, now crumbling edifices, and write my trenchant reports on them, but now I had a woman. Yet I didn't really care that my readers were unhappy with me. It's not my job to fill the gaping holes in these miserable net crawlers' empty existences. Fuck 'em, I said, let them complain.

It was the Saturday after she officially moved into my house. I hadn't seen the guys in about three weeks, which was a fairly long time for us. We had been planning an excursion into the old Michigan Central train station. It was absolutely beautiful in its heyday, but was now a twenty-story carbuncle on the skyline, Detroit's tallest see-through building. It had also been my very first building to explore back in the day, when it wasn't surrounded by a six-foot-tall chain link fence. These days, there were still ways in. The guys didn't know, but I was planning to bring Jenna along on the mission. A risky thing, I know, a real flouting of the Man Rules, but I didn't care.

We met up with Martin and Chip in the parking lot of La Colmena, a Mexican *supermercado* on the southwest side. Martin didn't seem like he gave a shit one way or another that Jenna was there. Chip had a different reaction.

"I love your hair," was the first thing Chip said to her. Not the usual Detroit deadpan "Hey," not "Good to meet you," or "What up?" Nope: "I love your hair." I have to say, it was pretty darn gay of him. Not surprising, I suppose, considering that he's gay. You might not realize that about Chip right away, other than the sense of style, the sauntering good looks, grooming, etc. Hmm. Well, maybe you would realize it.

"Thanks," said Jenna, pointing at his shoes. "Are those the new Onitsuka Tigers? *Those* are awesome."

Jenna, though there are only certain shoes she can wear, is a great appreciator of footwear. So right off the bat, they're talking about shoes and design and reality TV shows that they both loved, etc. It was like *they* were dating. I started to wonder what she saw in me. Especially since I had scolded her for not wearing thicker-soled shoes.

Martin and I looked at each other, not sure what to say. Although I was glad to see my girlfriend and one of my best friends getting along, it was weird.

"Hey you guys?" I said. "Want to head over there?"

"I just love her," said Chip. "She's just the kind of woman you need."

Jenna brightened. "I like to think so."

Chip is the kind of person who tells people straight off when he likes them. He's been known to change his opinions later and inform the formerly liked person of that as well.

"We've all been wondering if he would find someone decent," Chip said. "Or anyone at all."

I sighed. "Yes, I know Martin, in particular, has been very concerned about my social life." I looked over at Martin, bringing him in on the joke. He looked away.

Chip cocked a brow. "You know, Martin actually does worry about you."

"Yeah right."

"He does sometimes talk about things to me, believe it or not." He turned to Jenna. "It happens a lot. Straight men confide in me. Less macho pressure. Less judgment." His glance shifted over to Martin. "Sorry, M. K. Not trying to embarrass you."

Martin did not look pleased. "Are we going to do this or are we going to fucking coffee klatch?" he said.

Jenna made a "Yikes!" face, then she and Chip both broke out laughing.

By the time we trooped over to the train station, under the scariest viaduct in the city, a long low underpass of dark and wet and stink, something had happened. There was an event happening on the front lawn, the end of a bike race or something. There were cops around. We had lost our chance. Jenna was disappointed, but I was strangely relieved.

We went to Evie's Tamales for lunch, then called it a day. There was much yucking around between Chip and Martin and me, but Jenna got quiet and stayed that way for most of the meal. When we got back to the house, I asked her what was up.

"I want to have a baby," is what she said.

She might as well have said that she was raised by meerkats. "You *what*?" I said, for no other reason than to just catch my breath.

She sat down at the kitchen table and looked right at me. "I want to have a baby. And I want you to be the father of said baby." She pushed her glasses up with her finger.

It was like someone hit me with a two-by-four in the solar plexus.

"What do you think?" she asked, smiling.

"What do I *think*? I think we just moved in together and you're talking about us having a baby together? Are you fucking nuts? Shouldn't we get to know each other better?"

"I know you fine, Digger. I think I even understand you. I'm pretty good at figuring people out. It was really nice to see you with your friends. I know you'll be great as a dad. You have a full heart."

I caught a reflection of myself in the kitchen window. It looked like I was watching the goriest part of a slasher film. "No I don't. I'm not full at all. I'm empty. I'm kind of a dick. You've said it yourself."

"You can be both."

"Why are you looking at me that way? Stop looking at me like this is news that I'll eventually be happy about! Quit it. I am not happy to hear this at all."

"Okay." She didn't stop smiling though.

"Oh, so you know me better than I know myself. Is that what you're saying?" That was when I shut down, walked into the living room, flopped hard onto my couch and stared at the ceiling. Jenna gimped into the living room, sat down next to me, and placed her hand on my arm.

"I know this is a lot for you, I know. So we'll talk about it more later."

Rage was bubbling along the edges of my brainpan. All I wanted was her out of my house. "I don't want to *talk* about it later. There's nothing to *fucking talk* about."

She got up and left. So now what was I supposed to do, now that I had a crazy woman living under my roof?

For the next two days, I didn't talk to her, figuring she would get the message. No such luck. She hung out and acted like everything was cool.

I threw myself back into the Web site, posting stuff that I had been meaning to get to for ages—photos of buildings that we had explored months ago; a special page for "ghost ads," ancient painted billboards discovered on the sides of old buildings; party store murals; and spelunker video clips. Jenna had been around a lot, leaving only to go to class and to her job at the library. I kept wondering when she was going to get fed up. Meanwhile, Martin and Chip and I planned a night mission: the old David Whitney building on Woodward. Martin had heard about a way to get in.

Inside, the place was actually in decent shape, thanks to some casino office rehab a few years back. For once, it was nice to be somewhere that wasn't totally trashed. Of course, it's not like *we* mess anything up. Take only photographs, leave only footprints; we're down with that Sierra Club shit. Anyway, the view from the roof was amazing. At least that's what I heard. Martin and Chip went out for a look while I hung in the stairwell, trying to remain calm. I caught a glimpse of them standing next to the giant letters that spelled out the name of a man long dead, one of Detroit's early lumber barons.

"It's beautiful out here. Sure you don't want to take a quick look?" yelled Chip. He was usually pretty gentle when it came to dealing with me and The Imp. Martin had long since given up.

"No thanks." I heard traffic below and could picture the view as I leaped.

"Digga *please*," he said, exasperated. This was one of his favorite little jokes regarding my nickname. Sometimes he even referred to me as the "D-word."

Finally, Chip walked over to the doorway, took a look at me, and shook his head in disgust. "Damn. You are such a pussy. And when a gay man tells you you're being a pussy, you're a puss-*sey*."

"Whatever. This pussy's going down a floor. I'll meet you there."

"Later, pussy."

Eventually they got their fill and met up with me. I had found a good room with a nice view of Grand Circus Park, where we sat and drank pint cans of Guinness and nipped from Chip's hip flask of Jameson's. After a few pops, I didn't think at all about that star-lined bowl of darkness above me or the exhaust-dimmed streetlights below or the void in between. Although you think it would be the other way around, alcohol kept The Imp at bay. Depressants actually made me want to kill myself less.

"So what are you going to do about Jenna?" Martin said.

"Fuck if I know."

"She's a little baby crazy, but I still think you need to give this a chance," said Chip. "She's a good woman."

"What do *you* know about women?" I blurted, meaner than I meant to sound.

His pained look softened after a moment. "More than you."

The next morning, I woke up to the sounds of Jenna pouring granola from the box in the kitchen. It was shatteringly loud, as if she were up on a ladder, pouring it from thirty feet in the air into a massive hollow metal bowl and amplified through a wall of Marshall stacks. I was a little hungover.

Jenna shambled into the bedroom eating from a normal-sized bowl. "Hey dipshit," she said. Her eyes were wide and sparkling. "I'm sorry I freaked you out the other day."

"I think you should move out," I said.

Her eyes didn't change a bit. She just walked out of the room. I heard her eating at my kitchen table. Actually it was *her* kitchen table, which was nice to have around. I thought I would definitely get one after she got her insane baby-wanting ass out of my house. My other thought was: *shouldn't she be packing? I just booted her out.*

I had a freelance photographic job that day, just brochure work, but it paid the bills. When I walked into the house that evening, bone tired, she was still there and putting dinner on the table. Roasted chicken with rosemary and lemon, wild rice, and a mixed green salad. I wanted to ask her why she was still in my house, but I was suddenly starving.

"How did it go?" she asked, tipping a chicken breast on a bed of rice, then handing the plate over to me.

"Good," I said, too bushed to sound either pleasant or annoyed. I was thinking that maybe I could get into the moving-out part of the conversation after my entree. "The client was there and she was actually pretty cool. She let us have a little fun."

She smiled, pushed up her glasses with her index finger.

"I mean as much fun as you can have shooting spark plugs," I said.

Jenna let out a strange little laugh and then sighed. I took a bite of the chicken. It was so moist. I tasted lemon and the mellow evergreen tang of the rosemary. I'm not going to lie. It was the best chicken I'd ever tasted. Then I caught myself. What was I doing? Putting up with all this because I was hungry?

"When do you think you'll be moving out?" I blurted, almost out of breath.

She looked at me, plain-faced. "I'm not."

"You're not? This is my house. I asked you to leave."

"I'm not leaving," she said, shrugging.

What the fuck? I didn't know what to say. I just stared at her, trying to make her self-conscious. She yawned and lifted her arms, interlocked her fingers, forming a cup, then turned it inside out in that way I'd seen her do when practicing her asanas. She tilted her head toward the ceiling and closed her eyes. Ringlets of red hair played lightly on her shoulders. Behind her glasses, her eyelids were pink and almondlike.

I wasn't even sure I felt anything for her anymore. I don't know what I had been thinking letting her move in so soon. I admit I had been infatuated with her. Maybe it was because I had never gone into an abandoned building with a woman before, maybe that's all it was. I had not imagined that I could find someone who would not find this life strange and ugly, not find me strange and ugly. But there she was. She came to me now with a dish of blueberry crumble, holding a spoonful right up to my mouth.

"Just try it."

It was exquisite. Sweet and velvet warm. I dipped the spoon in the little jadeite ramekin and scooped out some for her. I put my thumb just below her lower lip and opened her mouth and directed the spoon in. She closed her lips around it and I pulled out the spoon, using her upper lip to clean the bowl of liquid fruit. Two triangles of blueberry stained her lip and I licked them off.

It was a few weeks later when Jenna told me she was pregnant. I hadn't been in an abandoned building in almost a month, yet I didn't miss it. I had lost my hunger for that sick, sad beauty. I can't tell you why it had resonated so deeply with me. When I had found the empty buildings, I'd like to tell you it was as if I had found myself, but that's not exactly true. Sure, I had long believed myself rotting from the inside out, but that's too easy an explanation. We're all rotting inside, but we all don't tramp around fucked-up old buildings. All I really knew was that I needed to go back one more time.

The Fine Arts building was going down. Word had spread fast among the explorers. There was some good news though, they were going to save the facade and build behind it. Same exterior, all new interior. Either way, soon there would be a fence around the place and getting in would be impossible, since people would actually be paying attention for a change.

I decided to go by myself, which I had never done before. It was a warm evening and the city was extra loud. All the humidity seemed to carry the sounds of drunken suburbanites roaming the streets. Detroit was that kind of city now. I suppose it was a good thing, but it didn't quite seem that way to me.

When I got to the building, the door was wide open. Obviously other spelunkers had had the same idea as me. Once in, I wasn't really sure what it was I came to do, so I lurched through the rubble, looking for a stairway. After I located one and started climbing, my Mag Lite decided to misbehave. I kept tapping it to keep it bright, but it wouldn't stop flickering. It was the first time I had ever been really scared in a building. The graffiti looked threatening to me along the walls of the stairwell. *Big Al Black KKK,* said one of the tags. *ESE,* said another. I was hoping I didn't run into Big Al while I was there. I made it up to the third floor and looked out from an office onto Adams. Someone was watching me from the street, wondering what that crazy white boy was doing.

I kept going up the stairs, my flashlight growing dimmer as I ascended, but still I kept climbing. On the seventh floor it took a little navigating, but I managed to find the door to the roof of the building. It was wide open. I walked out there and strolled right up to the half-wall that spanned the perimeter of the roof. I pushed aside the image of me leaping, soaring out over the street, to land with a hollow wet *foomp*. I took a taut breath and I looked out at the city beneath me.

Before long, I started to relax. First by focusing on the horizon, velvet black and studded with golden light; then on the darkened carcasses of the empty buildings I had explored—all that history soon to be gone. Finally, my eyes settled on the new buildings going up, their shiny exteriors, work sites mercury bright even in the nighttime, the cranes and other leviathans that moved earth and girders from one place to another. I saw that the old city was going away.

Walking back down the stairs, stumbling in the dim, I tapped my Mag Lite against my thigh and its sudden beam blipped me into brightness. It was then I happened to notice some cans of spray paint on the ground in the staircase. I picked one up, gave it a good shake, and then wrote my name on the cleanest wall I could find.

the lost tiki palaces of detroit

I was on the bus, heading down Woodward Avenue. We had just stopped at West Grand Boulevard and I craned my neck to check out the former site of the Mauna Loa. I probably do this once a week on the bus on my way to work. I try to imagine how the place must have looked there in the New Center: a massive Polynesian temple, its thatched A-frame entryway flanked by flaming torches and swaying winter-proof palm trees on a gently rippling man-made lagoon—nestled among the cathedrals of twentieth-century V-8 Hydromatic Commerce, just across the street from where they decided the pitiful fate of the Corvair.

I have an extensive collection of tiki mugs. My rarest are from the Mauna Loa. I own the Polynesian Pigeon, a section of ceramic bamboo with an exotic bird for a handle. Also the Baha Lana, an ebony tiki head sticking his tongue out at the drinker. Both say *Design by Mauna Loa Detroit* on the bottom.

There were high hopes for the place. It was to be the largest South Seas supper club of its kind in the Midwest. (Second only to the majestic Kahiki of Columbus, Ohio, now fallen to the wrecking ball since greedy owners sold to Walgreen's.) Over two million dollars were spent on this paradisiacal bastion of splendor, a lot of money in the late sixties.

There were five different dining rooms at the Mauna Loa (Tonga, Papeete, Bombay, Lanai, and one other that I forget), as well as the lavish Monkey Bar, which featured a Lucite bar-top with 1,250 Chinese coins embedded in it and bar tables made from brass hatch covers from trading schooners. A waterfall scurried down a mountainette of volcanic lava into a grotto lush with palm trees and flaming tikis. The waiters wore Mandarin jackets and turbans as they served you.

The Mauna Loa opened in August of 1967. Barely a month after the worst race riot in Detroit's history. It lasted not quite two years.

"I'm invisible!"

That's what the homeless man on the bus keeps saying. He boarded at West Grand Boulevard and none of us dared look at him. But then you never look anyone in the eye on the bus. All gazes are cast peripherally, on the down low. With the homeless man, we simply examined the air around him. Even the bus driver, a large man, blue-black and stoic, who never says more than a word or two to anyone as they board, looked away as the guy paid his fare. We all knew someone got on, but we weren't sure *who* it was. He could be smelled but not seen. The homeless man must have walked down the aisle defiantly, as if daring anyone to say something to him.

"That's right! I'm invisible!"

What could we say? We had all looked away. *We* made him invisible.

I was pretty sure that he was sitting three aisles up from me on the other side. The bus wasn't nearly as full as it usually was on a Monday—President's Day or some such nonsense. I kept my eyes on my newspaper, but they kept straying out the window searching for landmarks, lost ones as well as those still standing. I gazed upon a beautiful old abandoned factory from the twenties, with a sign that read:

AMERICAN BEAUTY ELECTRIC IRONS

I kept my ears open. I felt the homeless man's eyes on me. I wanted to look, but didn't want him to catch me looking because I wasn't sure what he would say. When I felt his eyes leave me, I glanced forward into the bus, at the spaces around him.

A little boy, about two years old, sitting in the seat in front of him, was the only one that truly acknowledged the homeless man's existence. The little boy looked over the back of the seat at the homeless man, and started playing peek-a-boo with him. The man cracked a bitter half-smile at the child. Then he said it again:

"I'm invisible!"

I was frankly kind of impressed that the guy would say something like this. I don't expect a homeless guy on the bus to say such things, strange and existential—an awl to the heart. It made me think—*he understands his condition.* I thought about Ralph Ellison. The homeless guy looked around and repeated it yet again as he looked around at the rest of us on the bus.

The bus driver turned, scowled, but said nothing.

I looked away just before the homeless man saw me looking. He knew I had looked. Luckily, the child distracted him again. When I looked back, I saw him smile again at the child, wider this time, a grisly green and yellow smile, the school colors of the university we were now passing.

Then the child's mother, reading her own paper, realized what had been going on. She sat the little boy straight down in his seat, flashing a harsh glance behind her.

This set him off. His gestures suddenly grew more animated. It was if he had decided he would show us what an invisible homeless man on a city bus could do. He pointed out the window at a young woman in a short skirt and yelled to everyone in the bus:

"Look at the titties on her! Lookit them titties! Let me off!"

The bus didn't stop. Everybody stayed quiet. An older man across the aisle from me sighed and looked out the window. A cane was leaned against the empty seat next to him.

As we continued down Woodward, we approached the Fox Theatre. A block or two behind it, down Montcalm, I could catch a glimpse of the old Chin Tiki. By all rights, I should not be able to see three blocks behind a major building to spot another, but behind the Fox, save for a fire station and an abandoned party store, there are mostly empty fields, now used for parking for the new stadiums, baseball and football, on the east side of Woodward. For that moment, I can see the Chin Tiki's Polynesian facade, its doorway arched and pointed, the shape of hands praying. To whom? Some great invisible Tiki God? Perhaps Chango: god of fire, lightning, force, war, and virility.

That would be a good guess. For Marvin Chin actually opened his tiki bar when the riots were going on, around the same time as the Mauna Loa. Fires were everywhere in the city then, but not at the Chin Tiki. It would survive to become quite the popular place. Our parents ate there (when they dared venture downtown), as well as the stars: Streisand, DiMaggio, Muhammad Ali.

It held on until 1980, when it too closed up. But unlike the Mauna Loa, which suffered an ignoble end as a lowly seafood restaurant that eventually burned to the ground, the Chin Tiki was simply shuttered, all its Tiki treasures packed up and mothballed inside. To this day, it is still sealed up, a Tiki tomb of Tutankhamen, still owned by the Chin family, who are supposedly waiting it out, waiting for the inevitable gentrification. It will happen. Or it will become another parking lot. In the meantime, the place had a brief resurrection when Eminem used it to film a scene for *8 Mile*.

Chango works in mysterious ways.

"Hey, white man!"

Without thinking, I turn and look at the homeless man. Apparently, I'm not so invisible to him.

"What you doing here?"

Everyone on the bus is obliquely looking at me now. I have to say something.

"I'm going to work," I reply, coolly.

"What you on our bus for?"

"I'm just going to work," I repeat, then turn away and look out the window at the old Tele-Arts. It was a newsreel theater in my mother's time, but now it's been turned into some sort of swanky nightclub.

"Motherfucker on our bus."

"Shut your mouth," says the woman with the child in front of him. She's not sticking up for me, I know. She means that language in front of her child.

"Motherfucker."

Slowly she turns back to him, eyes like smoldering carbon. "You want to be invisible? I'll *make* you invisible."

She says it in that way that many black women have, that way that makes most anybody shut up if they know what's good for them. It certainly works on me, not that I invite that sort of thing. I mind my own business. It's the only way to be when you're the only white person on the bus, *the cue ball effect,* as a friend of mine calls it.

The homeless man quiets down for the moment. We're farther down Woodward now. I look out the window at the storefronts, facades ripped off, gaping wide open into the street. They are being gutted for new lofts, many of them right across from the old J. L. Hudson's site, where the behemoth department store was imploded. It is now replaced by a giant new skyscraper built by a software billionaire.

When things like this happen, the world starts to pay attention. *Detroit is a city reborn! Back from the dead! Rising from the ashes!* They can see us again. We were always there, but transparent, the way you can see right through the exoskeleton of the Michigan Central train station.

To the rest of the world, Detroit was just a place where Japanese film crews showed up every year to photograph the house fires on Halloween Eve, a.k.a., *Devil's night.* Other than that, they hardly saw us. We don't even show up on the city temperature listings on the Weather Channel.

Farther up, through one of the construction sites I catch a glimpse of the old Statler Hilton Hotel, once proud home of Trader Vic's. The building has been ignored for so long the windows are no longer even boarded up. The Michigan weather is not kind to a man-made tropical oasis. Inside, columns of bamboo once seemed to shore up rattan-wrapped walls. Glowing blowfish and a native kayak hung from the ceiling, along with colored globes encased in fishnets. At the front door, where a stoic Moai once stood sentry, there is rubble. Long pieces of terra-cotta tile still surround the front door, ragged with metal mesh, depicting the faces of tiki gods, mouths contorted, faces squinched into pained grimaces.

A Tyree Guyton lavender polka dot has now been painted on the door. He of the Heidelberg Project, a block-long art project composed completely of discarded objects: a gutted polka dot Rosa Parks bus, a backyard of vacuum cleaners, a tree of shoes. These dots appear on abandoned buildings all over the city. Cheery carbuncles that make sudden art of blight. What else can you do?

The story for Trader Vic's is much the same as the Chin Tiki and the

Mauna Loa. When the white folks disappeared from downtown Detroit at the end of the workday in the seventies, the clubs and restaurants foundered. The building is now slated for demolition, but it's been a ghost for decades. "Demolished by Neglect" as the preservationists like to say around here. They say it a lot.

I am chagrined to relate that I have been part of that demolition as well. One night, in a drunken tiki frenzy, some friends and I brought crowbars to this very site and ripped terra-cotta tiles from the facade of the building. No one was using them anymore, right? That's what we told ourselves. It was wrong, and I knew it. I think of my offense to the tiki gods when I look at my filched tile, which now resides in my backyard. Shame on me, I say. Shame. Yet these agonies of all our pasts will soon be ground into dust in the middle of the night, the preferred time to start the demolition of historic buildings here in Detroit.

Down one street, there is a sign on the side of a car wash: HAND WASH TO THE GLORY OF GOD.

"Motherfucker on our bus," I hear the homeless man mutter. I really wish he would stop saying that.

We pass by more construction sites. Things are changing here. New buildings push out the grand old ones, like bullies in a big rush. When you go downtown at night there are people there now, suburban people, city people, doing things, spending money.

"Hey white man! Why don't you go back to Livonia?" says the homeless man.

I ignore him. Nothing bad is going to happen, for some reason I know this. Yet it alarms me when I hear a startled inhalation, a collective *huh!* roll through the bus. I turn to look at the invisible man and I see that he now has dropped filthy trou and is displaying his penis to me and everyone else on the bus.

Frankly, I'm kind of relieved. An act of aggression, but a harmless one.

"I ain't too invisible now, am I, motherfuckers?" he yells, waving his spotted peter at everyone on board. To be on the safe side, I clutch my thermos, figuring it will work well as a cudgel if I need to use it that way. Taunt me, yes. Piss on me? I don't think so.

Still, it's a relief when the driver pulls the bus over right next to a construction site, stomps down the aisle and tells the now very visible homeless man to walk his raggedy ass off his bus. *Right now.*

With great dignity, the homeless man pulls up his pants, turns, and exits. When the pneumatic doors close behind him, there is only the smell of him left. The woman with the child looks sternly at me. She is holding her child closely, protecting him, her lips squeezed tight.

For a moment, I try not to laugh about what just happened, but just can't help myself. She looks at me, puts a hand over her mouth, but soon her head is shaking and she can no longer hold it in. Everyone on the bus starts laughing. Up in the rearview mirror, I can even see the driver smiling.